The Ladies of Eyesore Towers

A Novel

by

Janet Hutcheon

This Book is a work of fiction.

Characters are a product of the authors imagination and any resemblance to actual persons is coincidental.

The Ladies of Eyesore Towers

One

It was a cold Wednesday morning in the village of
Inkwell, and from the village hall, sounds of the morning's class reached Dorothy's ears as she hurried
through the main door. She was late, but her earlier
temptation to stay at home would have meant missing
the chance to see her friends, so she had made the effort. Her special friends, almost her only friends, were
Sue and Evie and she needed to talk to them after their
dancing class was over.

Through the internal doors she could see the rest of
the group standing in a circle, holding hands. Bags and
jackets lay on the chairs around the bare cream walls.
Mavis, their leader, was holding forth. Panting a little,
Dorothy crept in, sat to change her faithful old brogues
for a pair of pumps, then joined the circle, mouthing
"Sorry" to Mavis as she took Sue's and Evie's hands.

The class was called *Music and Movement for
Mothers,* and though there were plenty of mothers in
the village and the nearby town of Crumbleton, most
were too busy changing nappies or stuffing puréed
carrots into little mouths to bother with classes. Now

renamed as *Music and Movement for Grandmothers,* there wasn't one woman there under seventy.

"Right ladies, let's conclude our session with the Happiness Dance." Mavis turned, her skirts swirling around her, and pressed the button on the recorder. All fifteen of her dancers listened to the introduction, vainly trying to remember which of their steps they should start with, and with which foot. Mavis clapped to the rhythm of the music. Two steps forward, two steps back, turn to the right and start the chain. Dorothy felt for Evie's hand but it wasn't there. She had turned to the left, and the chain broke.

"Stop, stop, who doesn't her left from her right?" Dorothy saw Mavis cast her eye over the room, presumably not wishing to alienate any individual who might feel picked on. No doubt Evie was going her own sweet way, as usual.

"Concentrate, Evie," Mavis said, not too sternly. "Are you tired? You look like a hooker after a long night on the tiles."

There were a few sniggers from those among the least aged who knew what a hooker was and Evie gave her most winsome smile.

"Let's start again." Mavis turned again to the record player and the three friends rejoined the circle and the dance began once more.

Everyone agreed that Mavis was a real find. Suitably trained to teach those of mature years, Mavis understood that creaky hips, arthritic knees and swollen ankles were the order of the day. Her dances, which she claimed to have designed herself, included no more than seven movements: walking forwards and backwards, turning on the spot, walking left and right, the chain, which foxed many, and lifting a leg without falling over. The class hardly taxed her creative powers but at least she made 50p once a week from all comers.

Dorothy, Sue and Evie were regulars. How those three got together no one could imagine. Mavis called them The Holy Trinity – Dot the Bossy, Sue the Meek, and Evie the Mad. They appeared to have nothing in common yet they were firm friends and must each have got something out of their odd liaison.

It was usual at the end of the session to meet in the café on the top floor, for a reviving cup of coffee. There, with the coffee machine hissing in the background, Dorothy led her friends to a table away from the others where they sat like conspirators working on their plan. They were going to pool their resources and buy a house together, for the company and the mutual support. The Care Home beckoned and a way had to be found to avoid this at all costs.

Sue groaned. "We had better hurry up or my son will have me in a Home 'before you can say

"how's your father." He's so eager to get rid of me. He dragged me round Sunnyside Home last week, telling me how superb the place was, but honestly, it was horrendous. All those people sitting in a circle with their mouths hanging open. I don't want to look like that until I'm in my coffin and then I won't care. They treated us to a meal in the dining room; it was disgusting."

Evie shook her head regretfully. "I know, I know, my Daddy spent a few weeks in one. Cabbage, mash and mince on the menu every day. He threw up regularly."

Dorothy had no time for these trivialities. "But would your son shell out a third of the cost to see the back of you?"

Sue gazed into the distance. "Maybe. It depends on how much a third would be."

"I hope neither of you think we could all fit into my place. I know I have three bedrooms but the one bathroom is very small." Dorothy owned her small three-bedroom cottage, thanks to her husband who had disappeared without a trace many years before.

"With my bowels? I must have my own bathroom," squealed Evie, tapping her silverish curls – dyed or natural, no one could decide. She was a petite, fey sort of woman who waved slender arms about a lot in an elegant manner because, as she said, it had always been her ambition to be a dancer. "A Care Home would be the kiss of death for me," she added.

"As it is finally for all of them," added Dorothy. "And would you not talk about your bowels please. It's not decent. Now, have either of you looked around and seen anything suitable?"

A bedroom each, three ensuite bathrooms, a kitchen and a large sitting room were the minimum requirements. They would split the cost three ways. Evie had her daddy's money, Sue was relying on her son's desperation and Dorothy would sell her house and put the proceeds into the pot. All that remained was to find a suitable property.

"I had details of a place in Marksman Close the other day. It looked a bit weird but it had all the things on our list. It's different from other houses and has been on the market for some time." Dorothy fished in her bag for the folded details and passed them round.

"Ooh, I like the unicorns on the pillars," crowed Evie. "Pity about the traffic cone though."

"You would think the agent would have removed it. Shall you go and view it, Dorothy? You could take some photos to show us next Wednesday." Sue handed the paper back to her, observing that the price was manageable, even surprisingly cheap.

The agent, Miss Minnow, admitted that the house had not been viewed for some months but she had done her best to present it to Dorothy in the best possible light. As they stood together on the drive, she enthused about the oriental touches, the overhanging roof, the coloured tiles with little curlicues at the corners. "So original, don't you think?"

"I was thinking more Gothic, myself," offered Dorothy. "Those pointy windows and the arched doorway, you know."

"Interesting, so interesting," mused Miss Minnow. "Quite an architect's dream, I should say."

The word *nightmare* flitted across Dorothy brain. A hotchpotch of stylistic blunders, was her opinion. "Let's have a look inside, then."

The living room that led off the hall was vast, quite large enough for three people to sprint around, should they feel like sprinting. The kitchen was dated but would serve, and there was a boot room, a cloakroom and a conservatory where a green light filtered through the mould-covered glass, giving the space a mysterious biological ambiance.

"Mmm, is the damp on the outside or the inside?" she asked.

Miss Minnow was not sure, but wherever it was, a jet spray would solve the problem.

The three bedrooms were large and each had their own individual distinction, due in part to the bizarre wallpaper on all the walls. Huge poppies adorned one, a yellow and green mosaic design in the second was enough to give an occupant a migraine if they should be fool enough to stare at it for too long. The third had wavy stripes in blue and pink inviting a faint seasick sensation. Each room had its own bathroom complete with a willow-patterned lavatory bowl and a cast iron roll-edged bath that the ladies agreed would not do. Dorothy, being over six feet tall, might cock her leg over to get in, but Evie would never manage to get either in or out without risking life and limb.

"Sensational, don't you think?" said Miss Minnow, mindful of her commission, as she closed the stained glass panelled door as they left. "And such a bargain. Of course, a few repairs and a little updating are required to bring it up to modern standards, unless its original features are to your taste."

As instructed, Dorothy had taken several photographs on her phone. "I shall have to talk it over with my colleagues and let you know."

Miss Minnow gave her a lift into town and, needing a cup of tea before catching the bus home, Dorothy went into Marks and Spencer to think. There were a number of important questions she had omitted to ask the agent, and she cursed her failing memory. How did the previous owners heat the place? Was there gas, oil or electricity? How about mains drainage, and where was the nearest bus stop? Was it freehold and did the roof leak? Her friends were bound to ask and all she had to enlighten them were a few photographs.

The following Wednesday, after they had tripped the light fantastic and endured a cooling off period of deep breathing and stretching, hardly necessary since no one ever broke into a sweat during their dances, the three friends climbed to the café. Dorothy described the house as well as she could. "It's different, I'll say that, and it's old and neglected, but there's lots of room. Its main virtue is the three bathrooms. That is unusual in a vintage property. And we would have to smarten it up a bit, of course."

"We could sort it out, make changes at our leisure, don't you think?" asked Sue, looking afraid she had talked out of turn.

"I think so, assuming we could afford to do the work," Dorothy replied

"Well, I'll tell you now," said Evie, "I don't climb ladders any more and my carpentry skills need improvising." Evie, unaware of her verbal blunder, put her hands with their three-quarter-inch blue nails on the table to prove the point, treating them all to a winning smile.

Then the "what about" questions started. What about the garden? What about the windows, are they double glazed? Was it on mains drainage? They couldn't be doing with one of those cess pit things.

Dorothy admitted the garden was a virtual wilderness with a few cankered fruit trees and a threadbare lawn. "Very right-on for the wild life in the present climate." she said. "The windows are unlikely to be double glazed and the other houses in the Close must have modern sewage disposal. Those I saw are owned by some of the posher sort, I suspect, so we would have nice neighbours, which is in its favour." Dorothy did like to mix with the better sort of person. "We could give it an attractive name at the very least."

Enthusiasm was warming among their small group and the upshot was the three of them agreed to go together to give the house a second look.

The taxi crawled along Marksman Close, past the pristine villas, all white and shining in the sunlight. It drew up at the last house on the right and the three got out, the optimistic smiles fading from their faces. Miss Minnow was waiting at the gate. Dorothy shook her hand and introduced her companions.

Sue was dismayed. The sight was even worse than the photographs Dorothy had shown them and even they were not exactly top notch. Under her breath she murmured, "Gosh, what an eyesore."

"I like it," said Evie. "It's different. It's nice to be ori…ori, origemenial and stand out from the crowd. We can call it Eyesore Towers," she quipped.

Their laughs were half-hearted but, having made the journey, the three felt duty bound to join Miss Minnow for her second guided tour.

They passed the stone pillars on either side of the gate, topped with the stone unicorns. One still sported a traffic cone in lieu of its horn that Miss Minnow said had suffered blunt force trauma by some young prankster months before. They walked the short drive to the front door and Dorothy tapped the stained-glass panel. "It's quite ecclesiastical, isn't it – reclaimed from some defunct church, I suppose."

Miss Minnow shrugged.

They walked around the empty rooms, their voices echoing into the silence. They passed a huge stone fireplace in the main room. Miss Minnow pointed. "That is French, you know."

Evie, in a fever of delight at all the floor space, skipped and shimmied, pirouetted and entrechat-ed up and down the room to some music only she could hear. "I love it already," she breathed, her chest heaving in ecstasy.

Sue examined the kitchen. Plenty of space but not much in it. She wasn't over-fond of big kitchens that required a thirty-second walk across the room to open the fridge door, and thirty seconds to walk back to whatever was boiling over. There was no fridge or freezer that she could see or anything at all except lots of cup hooks and a shelf or two. Still, that was better than a collection of defunct appliances.

Dorothy tutted all the way up to the bedrooms and even more sharply when they trooped into each one. Evie claimed the giant poppies, Sue thought she might put up with the stripes, leaving the mind-numbing mosaic for Dorothy. All were in agreement about the baths. Climbing in and out would be a perilous exercise at their ages and anyway the water cooled too quickly in a solid metal bath. Evie decided on the spot that she wouldn't be bathing until a shower was installed.

When they had seen everything, they stood in the hall to thank Miss Minnow.

Outside on the step, Dorothy said, "You know, we are behaving as if we had already decided on this house. We are running ahead of ourselves. We must talk about this carefully before making a decision." The glint of enthusiasm died in Evie's eyes but Sue agreed, nodding sagely. "I think we should each make a list of the pros and cons before next Wednesday. Don't you agree?"

They did and they would.

Two

Sue went back to the house she had lived in all her married life. She had been happy. Even when Alzheimer's robbed her husband of all coherent thought, she was content to minister to his bizarre needs until the Grim Reaper took him off. Of course, it had been her son's home too, and still was, but when he married Flora and they couldn't afford to buy, she suggested they live with her. The house was too big for her to manage and she would enjoy the company. He agreed and she felt pleased with herself for being a good mother.

The three of them managed a couple of months, long enough for the novelty to wear off. Flora was difficult and Sue knew she complained to Jerry. He would catch Sue when Flora wasn't around, looking harassed, and making suggestions. Could Sue not buy sugary cereals as Flora didn't eat sugar? Please would she not take the newspaper into the bath because Flora hadn't read it? Would Sue not talk to Flora when she was on the computer? Flora made her resentment clear, declaring that Sue was assuming too much togetherness. Things came to a head when Sue forgot to pass on a phone message, leaving Flora in trouble with the charity shop where she worked.

She remembered that painful day very well. Jerry had caught her after lunch just as she was settling for a nap. "Mum, we've got a proposal to put to you. Flora thinks the three of us all mixed up together in the house is… awkward. Why don't we split it so that we both have separate apartments? Then we won't need to bother you."

Upset and guilty, how could Sue refuse such a good idea? A separation would mean she no longer had to bear Frightful Flora's sulks and silences whenever Sue joined them. The woman was a bespectacled hippie type, all hoop earrings and scarves tied creatively around the neck Sue itched to strangle. She favoured long embroidered skirts that tinkled as she moved. She was Gypsy Rose Lee and a Hungarian peasant rolled into one.

It soon turned out that Flora had a better idea, and poor Jerry had crumpled beneath his wife's determination. He sidled into the kitchen, trailing a hand over the table top. "If you made the house over to us, Mum, I will pay the fees to the Sunnyside Retirement Home or any other you choose, for the rest of your life. After all, you don't need the responsibility of this place, and one day you are going to need looking after, aren't you?"

Sue looked at him for a long moment. He was fidgeting and sheepish. She had hoped that the couple would be around to look after her when that time came, but now that had become a terrible idea. "I'm only seventy-six and I enjoy my independence. I don't want to live in a Care Home."

"It's not a Care Home, Mum—Sunnyside is a Residential Home. That's quite different. You'll enjoy it."

Compliant to a fault, and sensing the pressure her poor son was under, Sue reluctantly gave way and agreed, not because she wanted to, but because she felt so sorry for him. He was thirty-four and already he was losing his hair.

Jerry was an accountant and some calculations had to be made: the value of the house, the Home's fees and the number of years Sue could be expected to survive. Sue was aiming for a hundred years, or at least ninety. That made almost thirty years. Thirty times the annual fees, whatever they were, might not leave Jerry a substantial profit, but the house could be expected to increase in value over that time. Of course, he denied he was eager to shift her but soon the pile of brochures was enough to paper the hall.

Thinking on it, to live independently with two pleasant friends was a desirable solution, so when the suggestion was made on that Wednesday morning about pros and cons, Sue's list mirrored her hopes. Three friends together would be fun, and any little differences of opinion would be bearable, so on her list there were more pros than cons.

Dorothy, being of a more acerbic nature, tended to emphasise the cons. "Look, the house is pretty run down and we will have plumbers, decorators, plasterers and carpenters tramping through for years to come. Do we want that? And can we raise enough cash between us? My cottage, when I sell it, will pay for my share of the new place, but will there be any money left for necessary repairs?" However, on the pro side, she had to admit she was fed up with her own company. When her two wards, Kitty and Clare, were growing up, she had an outlet for her determination to turn the girls into good middle class women. Her critical faculties were keen and she did her best to tame the little savages but both girls had escaped, Kitty into marriage and Clare into rural isolation, caring for an old man. On balance, Dorothy's list was more cons than pros.

Evie had no difficulty deciding. She lived alone in a small flat left by darling Daddy in his Will, plus a modest list of investments to see her through. The flat was cramped and she was prone, in a burst of flamboyant arm-waving, to knock things over. Not much given to housework, she skipped around the splintered photo frames, the shattered vases and the broken crockery, kicking aside the debris when she felt moved to practise her arabesques. The anticipation of waltzing around a bigger space blotted out any of cons.

In the cafe, Dorothy placed her flat white on the table, pulled up a chair and hung her bag on the back. "Okay, let's see what we've got."

Sue, always early, was seated and already half way through her cappucino. When Evie came back from the Ladies, they totted up the pros and cons while she sipped her latte.

"There is a surer way of doing this. We'll find the average. I once got a prize for arithmetic when I was in school." Sue tried not to look smug.

"Oh yes, how many years ago was that?" Dorothy enquired.

"I can't remember. I guess I was about ten at the time."

There were groans around the table. "Okay, if you must."

Sue scribbled on the back of her shopping list. "Eighteen divided by three makes six. Thirteen divided by three makes four and a bit. There, that's clear enough. The pros have it."

A sigh of relief went round the table. Dorothy shook her head. "I hope we don't have this rigmarole every time there's a decision to be made."

There were cries of "Of course not." They knew this was the most crucial decision they would ever have to make and they had to get it right.

There was some talk then of what the next step should be. Dorothy wanted to negotiate a lower offer in view of all the work that had to be done. She suggested that she herself should take on this chore. "I had better do it. Both of you are not as tough as I am." She knew that Evie was devoid of critical faculties and Sue would follow what everyone else did, taking any stance that avoided confrontation.

Evie giggled. "You know me, I'll agree to anything." And Sue nodded in agreement.

So the dye was cast. They were going to cock a snook to all critics and live together in peace and harmony.

Three

In all the excitement of having their offer accepted, the ladies forgot about a survey and went ahead with the purchase of what they now jokingly called Eyesore Towers. To make matters even better, Miss Minnow lowered her commission. For her it was a relief to get shot finally of that blemish on the face of the Close. The money saved was spent on a cleaning company that went through the house from top to bottom in readiness for the new occupants. The ladies were given a moving date, sufficiently far ahead to give them time to debate whether they had done the right thing. They asked themselves if they had thought long and hard enough, because when the money was paid there was no going back. Evie had cashed in her investments. Jerry had taken out a loan, and moaned about the rate of interest. Dorothy took so long to find a buyer for her cottage that she had to lower her asking price and now there was hardly any cash left. They were going to live on three old-age pensions, but excitement was still running high. They were going to live frugally together, free and independent, as they had planned.

The contents of Evie's flat and all that was in Dorothy's house were relocated to appropriate rooms in the new house. Sue thought it only fair to leave all the furniture and fittings in her erstwhile home to Jerry and Flora by way of recompense for the great financial burden she had landed them with, even though she learned Jerry soon expected promotion in Frogerty's Feather Factory, where he counted the beans. However, she surprised them both by insisting on keeping for herself the white goods which she argued were almost worn out. Flora would love a new fridge, freezer and washing machine, she told Jerry. Having laid claim to these (not very) worn items, she arranged for them to be delivered in the next day or two.

It was gin-and-tonics all round on the day when everything was delivered and *in situ.* The women were exhausted. Sue had done her back in, Dorothy's knees were giving her gyp and Evie had gone all vague. She drifted around, humming a little tune. Her contribution to the day's effort was to arrange the cutlery in the kitchen drawers, count the spoons and hang a mug on every cup hook on the walls.

By the evening they were all flat out. Sue lay back against the sofa cushions and asked Dorothy to ring for a pizza, declaring she had no energy left for cooking. While they waited for the delivery, Evie went up to her bedroom. Apart from the giant poppies, there was a single bed, bedside table and lamp and a Lloyd Loom chair with her pussycat cushion. As there was no wardrobe, she had to hunt among the cardboard boxes containing her clothes. She got ready for bed and, clinging for dear life to the banister, she made her way downstairs when the delivery boy rang the bell.

"What on earth are you wearing, Evie? You look like the unfortunate heroine of some old vampire movie." Sue was too polite to comment on the apparition before them, but Dorothy had no such constraints.

The garment in question was gauzy, floaty, almost transparent with frilly additions to sleeves and throat in a gloriously vibrant pink.

"It's my neglige."

"Don't you mean negligée, dear?" Sue said gently.

"Whatever," Evie waved a dismissive hand before executing a neat two-step and when the pizza had been consumed, she opted for an early night and glided to the stairs, cooing "Nighty night."

Dorothy and Sue watched her go. "What on earth can we do with her. Neglige indeed!"

"It's good that she remembers some words, even if they are not the right ones," commented Sue, thinking the best as usual.

Evie climbed the stairs on her hands and knees but it was a slow, troublesome journey as the voluminous "neglige" got in the way. She was pleased with her room when she finally reached it. It was almost a replica of the one she had left behind except for the poppies. There was even a collection of her favourite books on the bedside table; *Ann of Green Gables, Pippi Longstocking* and several volumes of *Harry Potter*.

Although she would never admit it, she was eighty-one years old and her eyesight was not what it was, nor was her ability to focus or pay attention to anything for more than five minutes, so the books were redundant. They were there simply to remind her of the halcyon days when the sun shone every day and she could do the splits and walk *en pointe* for seven whole minutes.

She missed her daddy, a lovely old gentleman she barely remembered now. Both she and her father had suffered much under the fulsome but misguided attentions of adored Mummy who had departed this life many years before, leaving Evie and her father to bond for his remaining years tighter than a duck's backside.

Dear Daddy, so loving, so generous, so proud of her. He had been both mother and father to her in those years, encouraging her in everything she did, no matter how crazy. His photograph was somewhere in the cardboard boxes. She would fish it out in the morning.

The first thing Sue saw when she opened the door to her room was her violin case on the bed. They had been so occupied with the lifting and shifting that she had forgotten it was there, waiting for her. Jerry and Flora had stopped her practising, not in so many words, but the plugged ears, the grimaces and their hasty retreat to sit in the car until she had done, said it all. She felt forced to give up unless they were both out, but it curtailed her mastering *The Lark Ascending* that Flora had described as "an insult to the idiot who composed it". Sue could never figure out why they were both such cultural heathens but she supposed it was probably her fault. Everything was always her fault.

In the room next door, Dorothy creamed her face, bending to squint into the scarred wall mirror that was for shorter people than herself. She eased the cream into the wrinkles around her eyes and at the corners of her mouth. She applied Vaseline to her cracked lips and took the tweezers to the one maverick hair that sprouted on her chin. Luckily the depilator had worked wonders above her top lip, an area that needed constant vigilance. And the fluff on her cheeks? It was time to get her Lady-shave on to that before it turned into a beard. The fecundity of hair growth in old people surprised her. Why didn't younger women have to resort to the tweezers, the razor and the stainless-steel nail clippers to keep their bodies in good order?

Her toilette complete, she put on her winceyette pyjamas then felt under the duvet. Was it too late to forage for a hot water bottle? Probably, but if she felt cold in the night, her old cardigan would have to do. Her mind went round and round. Would it have been wiser to accept that offer of a home with Clare, the elder of her two wards, when it had been offered several months before? At least that billet would have been sound and warm. Six people in that vast house, and she would have been the seventh. She had hesitated. She didn't want to be ruled over by Clare who would surely do her best to make up for the indignities suffered when she and her sister were growing up. Dorothy had gone to great lengths during those early years to bring the cocky young madam down a peg or two and had used a firm hand, in all senses of the word. She had taken some time to think about that offer but then out of the blue, it had been withdrawn. What was she to make of that?

It was the ladies' first night in their new home. Each one lay for a while, contemplating the day's exertions, all with the same hope she had done the right thing in the long run. The last thought Dorothy had before sleep overtook her was that there had been too much cheese in that pizza and indigestion was sure to follow.

The next morning, Sue was up early. She laid the breakfast table for three, made a pile of toast and a huge pot of coffee. There were eggs waiting on the hob to be cooked.

Dorothy came in from the garden. "I was up at the crack of dawn so I went to examine the state of our domain. We've got chafer bugs in the lawn, thrift in the hedges, canker on the fruit trees and black spots on the floribunda."

"I didn't know you were a gardener, Dorothy."

"I'm not, but I certainly know when things aren't right."

Sue frowned, "Surely we've got more important things to do inside the house. The garden is low on our list of priorities."

"Of course, I know that, but I shall put it at the bottom of the list of things to do."

"I had a gardener in my other place but he was a bit of a dead loss. I almost had to stand over him and tell him which weeds to pull up. Left to his own devices, if a weed was taller than nine inches he would replant it as a reward for its survival. I expect it was proud of outwitting his marauding fingers. I was sure he favoured the plants over anything I wanted to do."

Dorothy grunted. "What on earth are you burbling on about? By the way, what were these spectacles doing in the oven?" She pointed to the pink framed specs on the table.

"Pink? They must be Evie's."

At that moment, Evie wandered in, looking here and there about the room. This time she was wearing a fluffy white dressing gown covered in pink love hearts and mules sporting large pompoms, also pink.

"Looking for something, dear?" Sue asked.

"Ah, there they are," and Evie drifted over to the table and laid claim to her specs.

Dorothy frowned at her. "Why did you put them in the oven?"

"I did no such thing. Oo, what is that smell?"

Sue had opened her jar of Marmite and the distinctive aroma assailed their nostrils.

"Yuck, I don't know how you can eat that stuff." Dorothy pulled a face.

Evie sat down at the table. "Did you hear that cat last evening? It was so close. Do you think the last owners abandoned the poor thing?"

Dorothy levelled the knife at Sue. "I think that was our Yehudi Menuhin here."

Sue busied herself at the stove, keeping her lips tight shut.

"I'm going to fry an egg if that's alright," continued Evie. "I used to fry an egg every morning for Daddy."

"In that case, can you do one for me to take the smell of that awful stuff away?"

When her egg arrived, Dorothy looked down at it. It was covered in a yellow sauce. *Super*, she thought. *What a treat – eggs Benedict,* and she took a mouthful, only to chew and gulp. With a disgusted growl, she said, "If this is hollandaise sauce, I'm a Dutchman. What did you put on this egg, Evie?"

"It's custard. Is it too sweet for you? Daddy used to love it and I've got a terrible sweet tooth."

Dorothy looked at the Marmite to her left and custard to her right and came to swift decision. She would get up early every morning and eat her toast and peanut butter in peace.

It took a while for all the defects of the house to show up. The boiler didn't work so there was no heating or hot water. The cold water came out brown, dispensing dribbles in odd places from old pipes. The oven was temperamental and one of the hobs refused to respond to any kind of control. Things had a tendency to crack, splinter or break when touched. It was almost as if the house was denying them the use of its facilities, especially when a door knob came away in Evie's hand and she gave a little wail, "This house doesn't want us here."

At that moment, Dorothy was soaking her feet in the washing up bowl then planning to clip her nails and fit corn plasters on the soles of her feet. It was not exactly respectable to do this in public but needs must. The task required the contortions of a circus performer. She straightened up, reached for a towel and caught Evie watching her.

"Is that the limit of your beauty regime, Dorothy?" Evie said, grinning widely.

"Mind your own business and for goodness sake stop being so fanciful about the house. It is just like us, falling apart from old age."

"And neglect," Evie said, pulling a face. "It's short on tender loving care, like we are."

"Speak for yourself, you daft female. You should have got used to that years ago. Who wastes loving care on old biddies like us?"

"Maybe so, but we don't have to like it."

Dorothy gave a heavy sigh. "You are right. I never got much TLC from my husband. He lavished it all on his guppies. Took them with him when he left. Went out one day to buy fish food and crept back after dark to collect the tank. I hope he drowned in it."

"Oh Dorothy, that is so fu… sad. Did you never see him again?"

"No, and it just confirmed my view that they are all a useless bunch of no good dimwits."

"Guppies?"

"No, you dope, men!"

"Oh, I like men, I really do," said Evie. "My Daddy was a man."

Dorothy looked up to the heavens and heaved a deep sigh, but forbore to comment further.

At that moment Sue came back from her trip to the shops. "Who has brought in all that mud by the front door? I cleaned there yesterday."

There was a chorus of "Not me."

Ever the martyr, Sue pursed her lips and dumped the bag of potatoes on the table. "Now I'll have to do it all again later but right now I want a cup of tea."

"There's no milk, dear."

"What? Why didn't you say before I went for the spuds?"

"I don't drink milk," said Evie. "I'm lactose intolerable."

"I don't drink tea," added Dorothy. They both watched Sue's hunched shoulders disappear into the kitchen. She didn't say anything but she was clearly not happy.

Evie was sitting cross legged on the floor painting her nails a lurid purple. Without a pause in her concentration, she said, "What's the name of the stuff I use to take this off with?"

"Nail polish remover?" Dorothy pushed her feet forward and surveyed her handiwork with the nail clippers.

"No, the chemical stuff. I know it begins with A and I can almost see it in my head but I just can't get it out."

"You mean acetone."

"Yes, that's the stuff. My memory is worse these days. Do you think I've caught Alzheimer's from someone?"

"It's not contagious, Evelyn." Dorothy always used people's full name when she was being stern. "I don't know why you bother with all that rubbish at your age."

"I like to look my best. Don't you? Every woman has a beauty regime."

"I can't say I have ever bothered. I wash my face, don't I? And shower regularly – well, at least I used to. What more does anyone need?"

"Mm, that's why you favour the jumble-sale look, is it? No man wants his wife to look like a refugee from the workhouse."

"Well, I'm no longer a wife, so that's alright. Mind you, I hate to admit it but I used to get some lovely stuff for the girls from jumble sales. But I'll tell you this, if we don't get some more money soon, we'll all be first in the queue for any jumble that's going. I bet we are all going to look pretty shabby in a few months."

Suddenly alert, Evie complained, "I would look better if you hadn't washed my best red skirt with that blue tablecloth. That's why I'm using purple garnish on my nails."

"I didn't do that!"

"Yes you did."

"It was you who ran in and shoved it in at the last minute."

"I never run anywhere these days. My sciatica won't let me."

"Okay then, you jigged in."

Sue stood in the doorway, red in the face. "Will you two stop arguing. You are doing my head in."

Witheringly, Evie stuck her nose in the air and said, "Dotty is just being her usual critical self."

Dorothy stamped her bare feet on the floor and hollered, "Don't call me Dotty."

"Don't you raise your voice to me. You called me The Sugar Plum Fairy the other day and I didn't shout at you."

Dorothy hauled herself out of the chair and with tight lips, stalked from the room, pushing carelessly past Sue as she went by.

Sue came in and sat in the empty chair. "So much for peace and harmony," and she folded her arms and frowned. "Do you think we should have it out with her?"

"About what?"

"All those sticky notes she keeps putting up. *Don't touch this, Remember to clean the sink after use.* They fall to the floor like Autumn leaves and nobody takes any notice of them. And then there's the rotas. She never asked me about any rota and she's got me down for cleaning all the windows on a Friday and polishing the silver on Sunday afternoon. I didn't know we had any silver."

"I've never seen any silver or rotas."

"Didn't you notice, Evie? You are due to cook supper two evenings a week and wash up the breakfast things every day."

"Well, I don't mind the cooking but I'm anaemic to Fairy liquid. It plays hell with my nails. I should take no notice of her, if I were you. That's what I do."

Sue returned to the kitchen. The kettle took an age to boil and tea without milk was horrible. She leant against the work top and seethed. She had volunteered to walk to the shop, not mentioning that the creeping arthritis in her hip hurt so much. She hoped to stop its advance by taking lots of exercise but now all she wanted was to sit down.

The hall floor would have to be scrubbed again. She had done it yesterday and Dorothy had passed by on her way to the downstairs loo and, seeing her on her hands and knees, made a rude comment about what a good skivvy she made. Didn't Dorothy realise how hard it was to get down to floor level when necessary, and then get up again, giving a good impression of a crab? And now the two of them had denied making the mess in the hall where there was this terrible smell of dog poo. She would have to do it all again and neither would be around to help. They both had this clever knack of disappearing when there were chores to do.

And now they were having an argy-bargy about some silly thing. It was too much.

Sue made a mug of pale milk-less tea and went into the hall. The heap of their outdoor shoes lay on the mat. One by one, she picked them up and sniffed. One of Dorothy's elephantine boots was the culprit. Reacting to the stench, she stepped back, knocking over her mug of tea that she had placed on the floor. *Oh bugger*, she thought. With the offending footwear in her hand, she charged into the lounge and threw it with some force to the floor in front of Dorothy. "There, it's yours. You clean up the mess," she cried, then burst into tears and rushed up the stairs to her room.

Four

There followed a few days of tension. Dorothy wasn't talking to Sue, and Sue was on strike, claiming that they were all taking her for granted, didn't appreciate all the hard work she put in and their ingratitude cut her to the quick. She moaned to Evie, hoping to get her support but the woman didn't care and played down the incident. "We've all got to get on, Sue." She twirled on the spot, delighting at the swish of material around her calves and showing her drawers in the process. "Be tolerant. Forget all about it. I have."

"It's all right for you but if things get too bad, I am going to say something. She is so bossy, and treats us like idiots. I might even leave." Sue tossed her head, acting defiant, although she knew she never would dare walk out.

Dorothy heard of all these complaints. "Don't worry, Evie, I can cope with Sue. Where can she go? Back to her beloved son and Frigid Flora, or whatever she calls her? And she hasn't got a penny to her name; it was all put in the house. She's too feeble by far, don't you think? That's my view."

Evie, unwilling to take sides, relayed these opinions to Sue, who made up her mind from that moment on to toughen up and assert herself, so she stayed in her room a lot, practising how to say 'no' and scratching on her violin.

On Wednesday, they had a visit from a Social Worker. The woman bustled in and Dorothy introduced her to everyone, though she didn't look too pleased about it. Virginia, for that was her name, was a large woman, well-built, and plump. Sue took one look at her and decided not to beat around the bush. "*Golly, she's fat,*" she thought. The woman had an interesting hairdo, almost a shaven head with a tuft on top dyed green, not unlike a moth-eaten Mohican. Was she living on potatoes like they were? The woman eased herself into a chair and they prepared to listen to what she had to say.

"Well now, ladies, aren't you adventurous. I could murder a cup of tea." Nobody moved.

Taking her cue from Dorothy, who had been darning her pop-sox, Sue put down the book she had fetched from the library: *How to Say No and Take Control of Your Life* . Evie was musing on the book she had just finished, a romance from the Barbara Cartland stable.

Since no tea was in the offing, Virginia continued. "We like to keep tabs on all the old people in the parish and when I heard you had bought this place, it became my duty to check that this, ahem… lovely house… is appropriate for your needs. Most of our oldies are candidates for a billet in one of our Residential or Care Homes, you see, so this is a welcome change for me."

Dorothy sat up, prepared to set this woman straight. "Being shunted into a Care Home doesn't apply to us. As you can see, we three are hardly on our last legs. We are fully *compos mentis* and enjoying our independence. That is why we have chosen to live together."

"Yes, well, I must still check on all our registered grannies and geezers, so if it's all right with you, I'd like to look over your domicile and assess its suitability. I take it there are just the three of you here?"

Bemused into silence and doing their best to hide feelings of indignation, all they could do was nod. Dorothy got up and Virginia prised herself from the chair. Sue and Evie stayed put. Dorothy was the best one to deal with this cheeky madam.

The tour of the house was prolonged. The woman took longer than Evie to climb the stairs and they heard a lot of thumping from the bedrooms. Sue wished she had removed the bowls on the floor under the roof leaks but it was too late now. Three flushes were heard, setting up a water hammer in the kitchen.

Returning to the ground floor, Virginia tugged at the wobbly banister, saying, "That's not going to save anyone's life." In the kitchen she recommended a rust-removal product and declined to sample Evie's latest batch of celery and beetroot cookies.

Back in the lounge, Dorothy did not invite her to sit and they both stood while Virginia stashed her notebook in her bag. She said, "You are going to need a lot of money to sort this place out. Is that going to be a problem for you all?"

With a dismissive gesture Dorothy said, "Oh, not at all. We have plans all lined up. Of course, it will take some time – workmen can be very unpredictable."

The woman pulled her cardigan more tightly around her. "It's not very warm in here. All the radiators are cold, I notice."

"Ah yes, we are having a little problem with the boiler but the engineer is due any day." Dorothy smiled her most ingratiating smile and coughed to cover the snort Evie had given at the mention of the boiler. "We light the fire in the evening if necessary, but we are a hardy lot, aren't we, girls?" She turned to look at her two friends, inviting them with a fierce glare to agree. Wan smiles were all they could manage.

"And you all get along? No quarrels, no arguments?"

"Good heavens, no. We are firm friends, have been for years and we have so much in common, don't we?" She turned to them again, a steely glint in her eye this time. They both nodded furiously.

"And wouldn't you rather have a warm room, all meals provided, no chores to do and a programme of lovely activities to share with lots of friends?"

Dorothy laughed a dry laugh, which provoked a false giggle from Sue and Evie. "Goodness me, no. We like our independence while we are fit and capable."

When she had gone, they had a review of the meeting, trying to assess whether they had passed the test.

"You did very well, I must say," said Sue. "But what was all that thumping from upstairs?"

"She was jumping on the floors to check the joists, I think. She asked me all sorts of questions about the facilities. I told her we loved the baths but showers were on order. It was a pity you had your smalls soaking in the handbasin, Evie. Why didn't you put them in the washing machine?"

Evie looked vague. "I can't remember."

"She even opened the boiler cupboard but it looked too technical, so that was a blessing, but she was curious about the other door on the landing, the one we can't open."

Evie said, "Yes, I've wondered about that. Why is it locked, Dorothy? Is it a cupboard or a storeroom and what's in there?"

"I haven't got X-Ray eyes, dear, so it's a mystery that will have to wait; there is too much else to do before we go breaking down doors."

"I hope she doesn't visit again, although I'm worried she was not impressed. Will the Council kick us out if our domicile doesn't come up to scratch?"

Dorothy didn't like to admit she was worried about this possibility. She hated the thought of the stodge, cabbage and rice pudding, followed by a daily nap, with everyone in a circle, mouths hanging open, rehearsing for when they were finally carried off.

Evie said, "Perhaps it wouldn't be too bad. I do love a sing-song and they wouldn't be all women – nice to have the odd man around."

"Some of them are very odd indeed," declared Dorothy with some asperity.

Fortunately, the visit had pulled them all together and the former tensions had evaporated. The next day, there was a thud of the post falling to the floor. Sue got up to look and came back with a pile of junk mail and a letter. "It's addressed to you, Dorothy. Someone knows

you've moved. Virginia couldn't have written her
report so soon, could she?"

The letter was from Miss Minnow and it contained a
small key. Sue picked it up and frowned. The letter said
that the previous owners had left for Australia in a rush
two years before. They had taken some of their
belongings but had put the rest in storage. However,
since they were unlikely to return and had heard that at
last the house was sold, they were happy for the new
owners to have any of the items they had left behind.
The rest could be given away or destroyed.

Miss Minnow wrote that Miss Belladonna Pasti and
her partner wanted to divest themselves of the cost of
storage and would appreciate swift action as the red
demand letters were threatening court action.

"I wonder why they left in a hurry," Sue mused.
"Does she say what the key is for?"

"No mention of that. The letter is signed by Miss
Minnow, pp B. Pasti and G. Slapper," replied Dorothy.

"I know what it's for," announced Evie. "It's that
locked door on the landing. What a hoot. Do you think
we will find a magic wardrobe?"

"What on earth are you talking about? It's probably
just a cupboard," Dorothy said.

They all looked at each other, and agreed they had to go and try the key. They made it up the stairs to where the two doors were, to the left and to the right.

Sue put her hands on her hips. "I guessed this one was the boiler cupboard and the other one empty storage space."

"Okay, let's try and solve the mystery," muttered Dorothy."

They all tried, but the key did not work and the door remained firmly shut.

Dorothy stood back, frowning as she thought until her expression brightened. "I reckon it's the key to the storage unit. I imagine we can go and choose what we'd like from what was left behind."

"Of course, it must be that," Sue said. "Shall we go this afternoon? It might be worth the cost of a taxi. The address of the company is on the letter."

They had lunch. Evie made them an omelette with left over baked beans, sliced radishes and crumpled cheese straws with gravy, then they boarded the taxi. The old fellow driving was cautious and frustrated them all by travelling at twenty-five miles per hour. However, they arrived and climbed out.

Sue examined their transport with a jaundiced eye. "Would you mind waiting? We shan't be long."

"No probs. Take your time," the man said, settling himself into his seat for forty winks.

The ladies wandered over to the entrance and negotiated with the receptionist, who showed them to the correct bay. The key opened the roll-up door and inside was a muddle of dark furniture and a heap of unidentifiable junk. The only items of interest to them were a roll-top desk, two deck chairs, a book case and a tallboy.

"What about this TV?" Evie asked, stroking the cabinet top.

Dorothy pressed a candelabra into her hands. "You've already got one in your bedroom and this is ancient. Now, we had better get them checked for woodworm and I'm going to put a post-it note on the pieces we want. I expect we'll have to pay for delivery." She signed a form on their way out, woke their driver and prepared to leave.

Evie lagged behind, sidled up to Sue and whispered, "Can you see a loo anywhere? I have to go."

Sue heaved a sigh and enquired of the receptionist. Evie trotted off and the other two waited in the car.

After ten minutes, Dorothy said, "That woman is a nightmare. What on earth is she doing in there? It doesn't take this long to pee."

"Are you going to be the one to ask her?" Sue said, knowing Evie was likely to be rather too forthcoming with the details

"We thought you'd got yourself flushed down the pan," Sue said when Evie finally returned.

"Oh no," she replied seriously. "I got my girdle tangled in my vest and then my knickers…"

"Okay, okay, we get the picture," they both chorused.

Five

Every afternoon it became a habit to have a little nap "to let our lunch go down". When duly revived they would sit together and chat. Conversation ranged over what kind of women their former owners were, but mostly they talked about money and how long it would be before they might start on the showers.

"We really need a good plumber. It's a big job to remove three baths and fit three walk-in showers. It is going to cost thousands."

"Don't forget the grab handles and a pull-down seat to sit on under the spray," Evie put in.

"You've been watching too many TV ads," said Sue.

"We will have to do something to show some progress in case that woman comes again," Dorothy added. "We can't have her thinking we are destitute or she'll have us in Council care in a flash. But I know a man. He's called Stan and he works up at the Hall where Clare lives, near the village of Beenwell. He's gardener there so we might pick his brains about the grubs."

"Never mind the grubs. Is he any good at plumbing?" Sue cried.

"He can turn his hand to anything and he won't be as expensive as a professional. I'll ask my daughter if he can do jobs outside the Hall."

Dorothy had picked up her knitting but it was hard for the others to tell exactly what she was labouring over. Lately she had complained that she saw two of everything.

"There is nothing wrong with my eyesight," she had grumpily declared when challenged for failing to cut off the black bits when peeling the potatoes. Seeing two of everything was no disadvantage, she claimed. It allowed her to check one image against the other to make sure she was seeing accurately. That was her story, anyway.

Sue had shelved the assertiveness book and was now attempting a biography of Yehudi Menuhin, having struggled with *The Lark Ascending* on her violin all morning, to the desperation of all within earshot. People had often asked her if she was playing a piece of *avant garde* rubbish because they couldn't identify the tune. "You will when I've got it right," she would reply.

One afternoon, it was just Dorothy and Sue who sat in the lounge. "Where has Evie got to this evening?" Dorothy said, peering at her knitting.

"She's in her room watching *Last of the Summer Wine*." Sue turned a page.

"Isn't that a children's programme?"

"No, well, yes, you could call it that. She's got a crush on one of the characters." Sue gave an amused smile.

"Heavens, not the raggedy one!"

"No, the raggedy one is Compo. She's got her eye on Norman Clegg, would you believe?"

"What's so appealing about Norman Clegg?"

"She says he is sweet and kind and he's short."

Dorothy snorted. "That follows. Not a dancer, then?"

"No, though she did tell me that when Nureyev died, she was so upset she wanted to go out and catch Aids so that she could die and be buried next to him."

"Really! Did she know him? I mean, had she ever met him?"

"Goodness, no. She'd only seen him on the telly."

There was a pause whilst they both considered this.

A few minutes later Sue asked, "How is you...your, what is it you are knitting?"

"It's a onesie."

"Crikey, it will be midsummer before you've finished it."

Dorothy raised her chin and sniffed. "I shall save it until next winter."

"I hope we'll have proper heating by then."

Dorothy peered at the hole two rows back where she had dropped a stitch."Oh, so do I."

"What about this mystery room, Dorothy? Will we ever be able to open that door?"

"Let's get the showers done first."

In caring mode, Sue closed her book. "I think we should start with Evie's. She's going to fall getting in or out of that bath or stay smelly. Every time she whirls past me in those long skirts of hers, I think 'urine'."

At that moment Evie came into the room. "You're in what?" she asked.

"Oh nothing, dear, we were just talking about the locked door."

"So are we in?"

"No, not yet."

Sue got up and made for the door. "I'll just get in half an hour's practise before we eat."

"Oh lor, I can't take much more of that squealing," Evie said when she had gone.

Dorothy glanced up. "What with your little foibles and hers, my tolerance is under great strain, but we have to put up with them."

"That is no foible, that is a torture."

"You are a fine one to talk. Who puts custard on their eggs and falls in love with a fantasy TV character?"

Evie put her nose in the air. "I was merely expressing my individuality."

"Then I suppose we must let Sue express hers. Let us pray she improves with time or that violin is going to have a nasty accident."

Evie mumbled to herself, but then, spying Sue in the garden with a young man, she skipped out to join them. She had some good ideas to put to this gardener chappie.

A couple of days later, the furniture from the storage company was delivered. After Sue had laboured strenuously with the Mister Sheen, the roll-top desk looked beautiful. It was solid, with carvings of fruit and veg on the drawer fronts and the top. Inside there were many little drawers for pens, envelopes and writing paper on each side of a similarly-carved rectangular panel. It stood against the bare wall in the living room, glowing in Victorian splendour.

The desk would come in handy, they all agreed, for the accounts, the bills, answering letters and the to-do list. No one mentioned rotas, for those had cast a mantle of gloom over the women.

"Sounded too much like rules to me," Sue had said. "I thought we were going to stay independent, together yet not together, if you know what I mean. Can't we not have any rules and see if being fair works?" They all agreed.

Dorothy hunted in the local newspaper for a handy plumber. It seemed that most were specialising in leaks, taps and pipes, so she called a bathroom company whose Dave would come, cast his beady eye over the site and quote for the shower job.

He was a big, bald-headed chap who tutted and shook his head when Evie told him what she had in mind. The quote, when it came, made Dorothy blanche. How could they afford so much? It was an itemised document and there was more to be done than they had imagined. The shower tray, the tiling, two screens, sealing and fitting, shower seat, grab handles and the shower fixture itself, all came to an eye-watering amount. To do all that just once would surely bankrupt them. Three times over was quite impossible.

"Can't we sell the baths, Dorothy?"

"I asked Dave but nobody wants them these days. A small amount for scrap metal is all we could hope for."

Evie clasped her hands at the memory. "But he was a lovely man, wasn't he? So strong and so male, he quite made my heart flutter."

Sue gaped at Evie in disbelief then shut her mouth.

Dorothy looked sternly at them. "Look, get used to the idea, you two. We shall save, and keep on saving until we have enough for one shower and then we'll save for the next, right?"

"Oh alright, if we must, but in the meantime, can we get someone to connect up the washing machine?"

"I've already done it, Evie."

"So I can put my vest and pants in now, can I?"

"When you've got a full load, you can, but it's not economic to wash just a couple of things."

"You don't have to tell me that, Miss Bossy," said Evie, pouting her lips in annoyance and frowning at Dorothy. "But I've run out of knickers."

A quick burst of horror swept around the other two, as they contemplated Evie sitting there without the requisite undergarments.

Recovering quickly, Dorothy was more concerned to stop the dripping taps. "Drip, drip, drip all night long. It's a terrible waste of water. There is a leak under the sink as well."

"What we need is a handyman to do all the little jobs. That wouldn't cost too much. What about that Stan you were going to talk to?" said Sue

"I asked, but he said the job was beyond his competence; he meant the shower job, of course. I don't feel like asking again. But what do you say to my asking my daughter Clare for tea or something? She could see how desperate we are and pass the word along to her boss. The Hammonds are pretty wealthy and they could easily help us out. Clare has her feet well under the table, more like one of the family, and she could plead our cause."

Sue nodded. "It's worth a try. He can only say no."

It wasn't just a couple of leaks. Many of the windows were stuck fast and one of the rings on the hotplate didn't work. Worst of all was the horrible smell of drains in the kitchen.

"I've prodded and poked but I think the problem is further down the outlet," Sue said.

"I just thought you had something unspeakable cooking in the oven."

"Shut up, Evie. That artichoke and prune risotto you gave us was infinitely worse and I couldn't open the window to let the smell out."

"It's my turn to cook this evening," Dorothy said, "and I'll be in and out of this kitchen like a rocket if we can't get rid of that whiff."

"I love rocket. Are we having that?" Evie brightened at the thought.

"Sorry dear, but it will be fish fingers and chips with baked beans if you're lucky."

Sue was looking pensive. "We should have had a survey done, you know."

Dorothy grumbled. "What would it have told us that we don't know about now?"

"It's the things we don't yet know about that is worrying me."

It was decided that they could afford a handyman who would come and fix the little jobs – the leaks, the taps, the rusted window catches and the hob. There were also several light bulbs missing and the downstairs loo didn't flush properly. This was used mostly by Evie who, when caught short, could not climb the stairs quick enough. The bowl had been almost white when they moved in but lately the staining had to be seen to be believed. Evie said she liked it because it had a wooden seat and the wallpaper put her in mind of lots of tutus.

Dorothy frowned. "Tutus? I thought they were umbrellas."

The handyman they found called himself Odd Job Bob. He came on Monday and set about the list they gave him. By the end of the day, he had fixed the taps and the leaks, fitted all the missing light bulbs and loosened most of the window latches.

"Can't do anything about your drains, Missis. You'll have to call in my pal, Bunged Up Bertie. There ain't much he don't know about drains."

On Tuesday, Bob did not appear. His granny had died.

On Wednesday, he tackled the downstairs loo. "It's your ballcock, Missis. You see, there's your overflow and there's your backflow, but if your ballcock don't work, then your valve is knackered."

Dorothy was transfixed by his abundant nose-hair. "How interesting, but can you fix it?"

"Course I can."

Thursday was another no-show. It was his dead dog this time. He did half a day on Friday but they didn't mind too much as he fixed the hob at last. It took them some time to work out the cost of two and a half day's work at the modest price of twenty-five pounds an hour.

Dorothy and Evie were chatting as they washed the dishes while in the distance Sue murdered *The Lark*

Ascending. Dorothy groaned. "I don't know about you but my impatience is ascending further by the day."

"You told me to make allowances and I'm doing my best. It's hard because Sue is always on at me to stop jigging about. That's what she calls my dancing. I know I broke a cup and two glasses last week but it's in my blood, Dorothy. I have the soul of Margot Fonteyn, that's what Daddy used to say."

Dorothy handed her a wet cup. "To be honest, that can get rather irritating, you know."

"What about you, with all those Post-It notes all over the place? *Don't touch this. Remember to shut the fridge door. Dorothy's pills - Keep out. Please Flush.* I thought we were doing without rules."

"Mm, not working, is it."

Similar grumbles were taking place too often for everyone's peace of mind, making a mockery of their goal. If Sue dared to get snappy, Evie sulked. If Dorothy forgot herself and said something more than usually derogatory, Sue psyched herself up and frowned at her. If Evie cooked one of her star dishes, like her pilchard and orange fricasee, the other two feigned a bilious attack or swore they had food poisoning. Sue's solution to that problem was to take over all the cooking as long as someone else did the washing up, and then found she had to do it herself.

Evie went on jigging about with no regard for cups, vases or lamps. Dorothy gave up the sticky notes and dared to hope a routine would emerge in time. "We can remind each other when something needs doing," she said, crossly fishing her indigestion pills out of the biscuit barrel. "And we should get all our complaints out into the open. Let's have a regular house meeting and clear the air. All this seething and sulking is making for a terrible atmosphere."

"It's because we all have different personalities," said Evie.

"It's because some of us have standards," groaned Dorothy, forgetting to be nice.

"Oh, really, Miss nose-in-the-air, hoity toity. Sue and I are just plebs, are we?"

"Well, all I'll say is that I've never heard of anyone using a teabag three times."

Evie's eyes widened. "I was trying to be ecomical. You are the one always moaning about money."

"That's because we haven't got any."

Sue threw up her hands. "Please. Let's stop all this wrangling. We had a dream, remember. It will slip away from us unless we are careful."

They bit their lips and accepted her new role as peacemaker. The assertiveness book was clearly doing her some good because she had said 'no' a few times lately and the sky hadn't fallen in. Nevertheless, after their discussions, it was a nasty shock when they exiled her to the garden shed to practise her violin.

Dorothy was urged in a friendly way to be less critical and to curb her savage tongue. For the next few weeks, she bit her tongue so often she thought she would lose the power of speech. To her, being outspoken was a virtue equal to truth-telling but her conviction persuaded no one.

Evie, always used to basking in attention and admiration, was surprised to be told that what people told her, and what they said behind her back, did not always tally. It was decided that she should restrict her dancing to an hour a day and not flirt with every male who hove into view.

Despite feeling a little sore after these frank decisions, it pleased them all to believe they were back on the route to peace and harmony. The dream was still intact.

Six

As spring advanced and the weather improved, they managed without the heating. Relations were improving and during this calm period, they managed to pay Odd Job Bob in dribs and drabs for the work he did. Dorothy managed to scrounge a second-hand hot water boiler from the Woman's Institute. It held several gallons of water which they kept hot for much of the time, so they didn't have to boil a kettle three or four times a day.

Bob had become a regular visitor as there was usually some small job that needed doing. It soon became clear that Evie had taken a fancy to him. While he worked, she hovered, she made cups of coffee and of tea, she passed him his spanner or a screwdriver until she knew the contents of his toolbox better than he did. On the days when he didn't show up, she mooned about the house, lost in a romantic daze. Dorothy felt obliged to tackle her ludicrous behaviour.

"He's married, Evie. You are wasting your time."

Evie tossed her head. "I don't know what you mean."

"You realise he's even younger than Norman Clegg."

"Oh, you don't think I was serious about him, do you?"

"I hope you're not serious about Odd Bob."

"Mind your own business. You are jealous because I've got a friend and you haven't."

"You are making yourself look a fool. He can't possibly be interested in you. You are too old."

"Age is just a number. Who can tell where Cupid's arrow will fall?"

"Oh glory, wait till he sees your varicose veins and your wrinkly bottom. We don't want to put him off – he's too useful."

Evie gave Dorothy a scathing look. "Don't be disgusting. Trust your imagination to hit rock bottom."

"Well, at least it's not a wrinkly one," said Dorothy, almost laughing, while Sue, despite herself, doubled up with mirth.

"Why do you think she chases after Bob, of all people?" Sue asked Dorothy when they were alone.

"Search me. Perhaps he reminds her of Dear Daddy. He did up and leave her, and she says she still misses him."

"Did he leave her? I didn't know that. Where did he go?"

Dorothy tutted. "To the grave, dear. Keep up. Surely you had figured that out."

Sue was embarrassed. "Oh, of course. I was forgetting how old she is."

Evie was most upset to hear her companions being glib about what to her was a refreshing new interest. They were making fun of her, belittling the immensity of the range of her emotional life. Something sweet had entered her days, some focus for her dreams that seemed to scrunch up her innards with wanting. The others were cold and unfeeling, especially Dorothy. They were rooted in the here and now, obsessed with problems and everyday things while her heart went soaring out and away and she wanted to dance, dance, dance.

Seven

Dorothy shut down her phone to save the battery. "That's all settled. Clare is coming to tea on Thursday. We must do what we can to impress her."

"Okay, I'll put some effort in and make something nice for our very first guest."

"Oh no, Sue, not a good impression, but a bad one. We want to make her sorry for us."

"Well, that won't be too difficult."

"But she has to know that we are all getting along well, no grumpy faces, no depression. The house may be falling down and we are poor, cold and uncomfortable but we are nevertheless happy to be together."

"What on earth have you got in mind? Is this another of your clever plans?"

"Yes. She will see for herself what needs doing and relay her concerns to her boss."

"No need to pretend there," the other two chorused.

"Her boss has pots of money. He could buy this house three times over. If Clare could convince him of our dire straits, he might make a substantial donation to us."

"Okay, but why should we not look depressed by our situation?" said Evie, prepared to do her best at the acting and unable to understand Dorothy's logic.

"Because Clare would have the Welfare or Social people here like a shot. They would take one look at this place and ship us off to a Home before you could say how do you do. Goodbye Dream."

Comprehension dawned on all faces, but would it work?

"We can only give it a go. A warm welcome, a quick trip round the establishment and a frugal tea might be enough to persuade her. I might drop a subtle hint about the obligations of the rich towards those in need, and we are in need, aren't we?"

Sue doubted that subtle was in Dorothy's vocabulary but in their new policy of friendly toleration, she held her tongue and began to plan the forthcoming tea. Should she put newspaper down on the table or was that going too far? Perhaps a bare table would be best. Jam sandwiches might be a good idea and the cheapest biscuits she could find. It went against the grain to mess with the actual cup of tea but a couple of old cracked mugs would look sad enough.

On the appointed day the first thing was to remove the battery from the doorbell on the basis that they couldn't afford unnecessary items.

While they waited, sitting before their empty grate, bundled up in all the jumpers they had because the house was so cold, Evie said, "This room looks pretty bare. Where is the picture of my hero and the vases and the rug?"

"All hidden away," Dorothy said. "We haven't got the money for fripperies, remember. Could you cut up some newspaper squares for the loo, if you've got nothing to do? I've removed the toilet rolls."

Evie tutted and muttered to herself, "It's just one giddy experience after another," but she went off to find some newspaper that wasn't being useful elsewhere.

The banging on the door announced Clare's arrival. Dorothy introduced her, then asked her to come into the warmest room in the house. In the kitchen, the tea was laid out, cracked cups, plastic plates, and a dented metal teapot. There were some sandwiches and cakes and a plate of broken biscuits. "We find the local charity shops handy for some things," she explained. Clare was surveying the room with a quizzical eye. "Not exactly flush on mod cons, are you?" she observed.

"The house took up most of our savings but we don't mind, do we?" Dorothy looked at the other two with a bright but threatening smile. They chorused and nodded vigorously. "We are just glad to be together."

Evie said, "We'll put up with anything to avoid the alternative."

Dorothy glared at Evie to shut her up. It was not a good idea to actually remind Clare of any alternative. "Well, not anything, Clare, but needs must at the moment. Sit down, no, not on that wonky chair. Sit here and I'll make the tea."

"The house feels chilly. If this is the warmest room, I can't think what the others are like."

"We live mostly in here, don't we. We can open the oven door for five or ten minutes to warm us up." Once again she looked at the others for agreement.

"Haven't you any heating in the house at all?"

"The boiler doesn't work. We are saving up to get it fixed," Sue answered, putting on her rueful face. "Have a cup of tea to warm you up and then we'll give you the Grand Tour."

"Can't wait," muttered Clare, pulling her jacket more tightly around her.

Soon after, they all shivered into the lounge, passing the jam jar full of wilting daffodils and the blankets folded on three chairs for warmth while watching TV.

For some unknown reason, Evie had developed a limp and as they went up the stairs, she lagged behind, shouting, "You go on ahead. My sciatica slows me down."

The wallpapers made Clare take a step backwards and blink.

Dorothy urged her into the bathrooms. "We do prefer plain walls but that job is low on our list of things to do."

Clare put her head around the door to the bathroom. "Well, you can't say it's not original but goodness me, that bath needs some updating."

"Oh, we don't use them," said Dorothy picking up an old towel from the floor. "We old people find them dangerous to climb in and out of and they do need an awful lot of water."

"I have no experience of them. We have showers at the Hall, but how do you wash?"

"One day, when our ship comes home, we will rip the baths out and install showers. We just do the best we can in the sink, or a wash basin."

Back on the landing, Clare remarked on the bowl of water on the floor. "Does your roof leak?"

"Only when it rains," came the reply. There was nothing more to see so they went down, meeting Evie struggling up on all fours. "I've missed the fun, have I?

The bathrooms are really something, aren't they? Don't come too close, I'm last on the rota for the sink. As you can imagine, I'm dying to have a shower."

Dorothy beamed and patted her on the head as they passed. Evie was a cross between a sensible person and the Mad Hatter. Trouble was, one never knew which persona one was dealing with. "We are all going to do the lottery in the hope that a modest amount of cash will come our way, but we're not banking on it, so these jobs won't get done, maybe never."

"You are going to need a fair amount of cash to sort this place out," Clare said.

Dorothy gave a long hopeless sigh. "We are hoping a Prince Charming will come our way and in the meantime, we carry on and keep cheerful."

In the hall, Clare turned to face them. "Just think, if you had all gone into a residential place you'd have your own room, you would be warm and well fed and watered, with a garden you wouldn't have to keep up and all maintenance done by others!"

"Oh, no, how boring. We prefer to please ourselves. We all get on so awfully well."

"Do you?"

"Oh, absolutely. We are the greatest of friends, aren't we?" Dorothy turned for confirmation and saw Sue with her arm around Evie's shoulders."

Evie piped up. "Don't you know any Prince Charming, Clare? We've heard…"

Dorothy interrupted, guessing what the woman was going to say, which would cause embarrassment to sweep over them all like a pall. "Let's get back to the warmth of the kitchen. Would you like more tea, Clare? Another sandwich?"

"Eh, no thank you, I'm not too keen on mashed turnips and I ought to be getting back. Thanks for showing me around. I was curious to see the place. I do hope you will all be happy here."

"Come any time. Come when it is warm, although I don't suppose we will have managed to do much by then unless some charitable soul steps in to help."

They all trouped to the door to see her depart. Evie exaggerated her limp and winced with every step. Sue hugged everyone in feigned happiness and Dorothy gritted her teeth, although she wasn't sure why.

They had another house meeting to assess how things had gone.

"Do you think she was suitably concerned for our welfare and comfort?" Sue asked. "You don't think we overdid things? She scarpered quickly enough, and didn't eat one of your jam and sardine sandwiches, nor your pea-pod fairy cakes."

"That was my contribution," Evie said proudly. "I had one. I wanted to make sure I'd got the recipe right."

"Mmm," murmured Dorothy. "Myself, I could have done without the sardines. Or the jam. Or the pea-pods, come to that. Now we must wait and see what happens. I didn't want to overdo the hinting unless it put her off."

"I think you did very well, Dorothy. Much more and she would have smelled a rat."

"That reminds me," said Evie, "I don't want to warm you, but I think we have mice in the kitchen cupboards."

Eight

Two weeks went by with no word from Clare so they began to think their ruse had not worked. Things were just getting desperate when they had a call to say that Gordon, Clare's boss, was prepared to pay for one or two invoices for necessary work.

It left them in a quandary; how large could the invoices be? They had expected a lump sum to be spent as they wished, but now they would have to get quotes and check them first with Clare in case they were asking too much.

"Why don't you just ask for my shower?" said Evie.

"Because it is a lot of money and I'm not sure we dare ask for so much. She's bound to ask me why we haven't made the roof our priority. I can't lie that now we have no leaks," Dorothy replied.

"Oh go on. He can only say no. Clare is your daughter so she's bound to be concerned for her mother's welfare and keen to persuade him."

Dorothy fidgeted and looked away. "My adopted daughter actually," she said in a low voice.

"You said you had two daughters."

"No, strictly speaking they are my wards; two orphans that I chose to give a home to."

Evie and Sue stared at her. Sue said, "You are a dark horse, but how noble of you. They must be really grateful for what you've done for them and keen to help you now."

Dorothy pulled a face. "I wasn't a loving parent to either girl. Clare fought me at every turn and Kitty, the weak one, cried at the drop of a sharp word, and made me so cross. It was only when they both left home that I realised I should have been a trifle less harsh. I doubt they feel grateful for much."

When Clare had phoned, she had apologised for the delay in getting back to them, saying she'd had to pick her moment before talking to Gordon. *"That's what you wanted me to do, wasn't it?"* she had said. Apparently, he was upset to think they were so cold and would pay for the central heating to be fixed if they sent him the invoice.

So now Dorothy sat at the new desk writing a letter thanking him for his generosity. It was a weight off their minds. "We can get the boiler fixed ASAP," she told her two companions. After that, she started on their household accounts, but within half an hour she was spitting and swearing over the numbers. "Who has nicked the bloody calculator?" she cried. Since she did most of the shopping, it should have been an easy task but something always went awry. "What is this? It doesn't belong here." She waved a scrap of paper at them. "It says Piles squiggle Cream."

"Oh, so sorry, that will be mine," Sue blushed . "It's my haemorrhoid cream. I can't think how it got in there."

"Please remember, you pay for your own personal things. You wouldn't want to pay for my corn plasters, now, would you? Or Evie's nail varnish?"

"Alright, alright. Don't go on about it. It was just a little mistake."

Dorothy's irritable side had come to the fore. She started opening the little drawers and slamming them shut. Suddenly they heard her say, "Oh golly, look at this."

The centre panel between the little drawers had sprung open. Evie got up to peer over her shoulder. "Goodness me, what a surprise. It's a secret drawer and look, it's stuffed with papers."

At her words, Sue dried her hands and came over.

They took everything out and laid the sheets on the desk top. Some were postcards, some unopened envelopes and there were lots of folded letters. Then, because there were so many, they transferred all to the table and sorted everything into piles.

"Fancy all these sitting in there for all this time. It's years, isn't it?" Evie was holding an envelope to her nose. "It smells a bit fusty. Belladonna and her chum must have forgotten all about them."

Sue said, "They must have left in a tearing hurry. Once the desk was in storage there probably wasn't time to go chasing after them."

Dorothy neatened the pile of letters. "Depends how important they were. I can't say I would bother about leaving a few letters behind, especially if I was leaving the country."

Sue picked up one sheet. "Should we read them, do you think? Is it a decent thing to do?"

"Oh for God's sake. We have to know if they might want us to send them on." Dorothy ripped open an envelope and unfolded the missive inside. They watched her eyes scan the handwriting, just a few short lines. She frowned. "Well, it seems the mystery deepens."

"What is it?" they chorused.

"Listen to this," and she read it out.

Dear Bella, thank you so much for you ministrations last night. My mind has cleared and I think I have decided what to do. Your dedication to my welfare is invaluable and should I need you to perform again, I hope I can count on you.

Yours, Buffalo Bill.

"What does it mean? What ministrations and what kind have to be performed?" Sue looked vaguely around the room.

"I don't know, do I," answered Dorothy. "Some service Bella – that's Belladonna – did for him. But Buffalo Bill, that's an alias for sure; some twerp trying to hide his identity, I suppose."

Evie picked up another sheet. "Maybe this will tell us more," and she began to read. "*My dearest Gussie, your service is as good as Bella's. I feel so good. I want to see you again very soon. My wife wanted to know why I was so happy but I couldn't tell her, could I? Thank you. Your new fan, Robin Hood.*"

"These aren't exactly love letters, are they," said a bewildered Sue. "These women are performing a service which these men, whoever they are, find valuable. What do you think it was? Counselling? Or massage? Chiropody? Some kind of treatment?" She looked from one mystified face to the other.

Dorothy said, "None of those would require a client to be incognito. No, it must be something very personal for men and bound to be salacious, I'll bet. What about women; are there any letters from women here?"

They started opening all the letters until all had been read. There were none from women and the content of each was similar, and all from a variety of aliases. Then they turned to the postcards.

One by one they read these out. Some were from educated men, others less well spelled. The messages were shorter and more direct, making them laugh even as they puzzled.

Dear Golden Girl,
I cannot thank you enough for your wonderful service.
I can't wait to visit you again. Love from Sixpack.

Hi, Dommy, Feel super now but more power to your arm next time.
Thanks, BraveBoy.

Hello Sexy,
Never enjoyed it so much. I'll be back when the bruises are gone. I blamed the scratches on the cat.
Bye for now, ThunderBum

Dear Mummy, I've been a naughty boy again.
I need my botty smacking really hard this time.
Kisses from Babykins.

There were many others in a similar vein, some alluding to gifts for services rendered. Evie was giggling helplessly. "I bet I know what these women were. They were sex workers. Look at the names, *Thunderbum*, *Brave Boy*, *Six Pack* - these men chose their own names. How exciting!"

Sue and Dorothy were silent, staring at the papers strewn on the table and the floor. Then Dorothy muttered, "Why do you have to come to such an unacceptable conclusion? It would not be my first thought."

"So what would your first thought be, then?"

"Not S, E, X, I can tell you."

"Oh, you old prude." Evie got up and started capering around the room, singing in a loud squeaky voice, "Sex, sex, sex," many times over.

"Do stop being so offensive, Evie. It is not funny."

"Why is it offensive?"

"Didn't your parents ever teach you decorum? It's not nice for ladies to…"

"Oh, give over, Dorothy. It's as clear as day what these letters mean."

"If you are right, I'm all for throwing this… trash into the bin." She waved a hand over the papers, her face taut with disapproval.

Sue didn't think they had to do anything, as the correspondence was old, anonymous and Gussie and Belladonna were no longer in the country.

"It's all so vulgar," Dorothy declared. "I'll have no truck with any of it."

Sue had been reading all of them, postmarked from all corners of the county. "Hang on, don't you think they are rather funny. This one for example. *You are the absolute best. Babykins is crying for Mummy. Can't wait till next time.*"

"Is he the one who wants his botty smacking?" Evie looked at Sue and they curled up laughing.

Dorothy was looking sour. "I don't find them in the least amusing. I think they are pathetic and disgusting. We should take them to the police. Those women were running an illegal business."

Evie reached for another clutch of papers. "I think you are exaserbating, but look, these sheets are clipped together, and they are different. Just listen to this. Evie read out one at random. *"I know your dirty secret. What's it worth to keep it out of the papers? £500?"* It looks as if Bella and Gussie were being blackmailed."

There were more in this vein.

You have been warned.
Keep your eye on Twitter. £500 will stop me.
Usual place - 10.30 at the southern end.

You don't want wifey to know, do you?
Buy my silence with £1000 in used notes
to the cemetery at midnight. Leave bag on fifth
grave on the left.

They all looked at each other with wonder in their eyes. Evie held up the pages. "These are not the same. They haven't been folded so they have never been posted. You know what that means, don't you?"

Dorothy nodded as the truth dawned. "It means they were not being blackmailed. They were doing the blackmailing."

"Oh, I say, that doesn't sound like a good service," Sue cried.

"No doubt it was good for them if they could avoid getting caught, although who would have thought two women would be capable of such wickedness. I thought they were decent but it seems not."

Evie said, "Pity we don't know how old they were, although the older they were, the less likely anyone would think them guilty."

"True, true." They all nodded, and with that a silence fell while they all pondered.

Sue was still mystified and broke the silence. "Is it a porno business they were running, or blackmail or both?"

"Looks like both and both were illegal" Dorothy was quite sure.

"But were they successful, do you think?" Sue persisted: an idea was stirring in her mind.

"Probably, the amounts look quite modest. I expect the police would not concern themselves unless they demanded hundreds of thousands of pounds."

Evie added her opinion that no man who was guilty would dare go to the police. "They would pay up, wouldn't they?" she added.

They made a cup of tea while they considered the question.

Sue said, as they sat down, "Five hundred pounds is not much in criminal terms but we would find even that amount useful."

They sat with sober expressions and thought about what they had found. It explained why their former owners had run off to Australia so speedily. They must have been found out and feared arrest. But how had the women discovered possible victims? But then they realised they wouldn't have to look far. Their porno clients would expect anonymity and make fine targets. The two women would know the names and addresses of all their clients under a promise of confidentiality, and from these they could choose the most likely men to approach.

The ladies couldn't decide what conclusion they should come to. At first, they had been appalled, then disgusted and shocked, then intrigued and, except for Dorothy, finally amused. After all, there might have been some other reason for rushing abroad. A sick relation, perhaps, or an out-of-date visa. Maybe one of their clients turned nasty, who could tell?

"What should we do about what we have discovered? Did our neighbours know? They must have seen all those men sneaking into the house. Should we tell anybody what we've found?" This was Sue, always keen to do the right thing if she only knew what the right thing was. She went on, "I don't think we should tell a soul. We might get those pathetic men showing up at our door expecting services."

Evie's imagination was in overdrive. "I say, how exciting. It sounds like tremendous fun."

"Don't be ridiculous, Evie," Dorothy snapped.

Sue was smiling. "So exactly which part of the business do you favour? I would be afraid to face them."

"I wouldn't mind," said Evie. "I'm prepared to smack anybody's botty for five hundred pounds," and she burst into peals of laughter.

Dorothy's severe look sobered her. "Control yourself, Evie. These women, Belladonna and Gussie, have been exploiting people for money. It is immoral."

It was Sue's turn to look severe. "You are being very sanctimonious, Dorothy. These women were doing a public service. There wasn't one letter that suggested the men were unhappy with what they paid for. Quite the opposite, in fact."

"I agree," said Evie," and it might have been Bella and Gussie's only source of income and that's why the house has been so poorly maintained. I doubt you can make a fortune smacking botties."

"If they were as badly off as we are, I can see why they turned to blackmail. Perhaps we should do the same." Sue gazed thoughtfully into space.

Dorothy straightened the steel rods in her back and squared her shoulders. "Well you can count me out. The indignity of it would be more than I could take."

Sue protested. "Hang on, I don't mean the porno part; none of us would do that except Margot Fonteyn here, but we might have a go at the blackmail. I bet none of these men were exactly poor."

"Sue, I'm ashamed of you. How could you even think of it?"

"You wouldn't say that if we got five hundred pounds for it. We could clean the drains out with that, and no one would know it was us."

"Someone would be sure to see you, especially sneaking around in the dead of night."

"Belladonna and Gussie never revealed themselves."

"We don't know that. We don't know why they went."

But Evie had not heard this. She had gone off into a world of her own. "It would be exciting. The only thing we do is *Music and Movement,* and that is hardly a thrill."

Dorothy sniffed. "I don't expect excitement at my age."

"Then you can join the legions of old biddies wasting away in Care Homes, darling,"

Dorothy pointed a finger at Evie. "Don't you call me darling. I'm not your darling."

Sue banged her fist on the arm of her chair. "Stop it, you two. Peace and harmony, remember!"

Eight

Now, there was something more interesting to talk about than money and how to get some. Speculation was rife and each had an opinion to offer. Evie crowed with delight at the thought of the fun Bella and Gussie had enjoyed in the secrecy of these rooms. Dorothy's twittering on about ethics and morality and the descent of good people into criminality had no effect on Evie whatever.

"You are an old prudeypants," Evie told her. "Don't you ever read the papers? This is run-of-the-mill stuff in the tabloids."

"I obviously don't read the same papers as you. Decent people don't blackmail other people, nor do they visit prostitutes." Dorothy was on her high horse and determined to stay there.

"If they do, they keep quiet about it. In some countries, prostitution is legal, even encouraged. Haven't you heard of the red light districts? It's the oldest profession in the world."

"Maybe, but blackmail never is," retorted Dorothy, "and I will have nothing to do with either. Anyway, how come you know so much about all this, Evie? Part of your misspent youth, was it?"

"No, but I wouldn't regret it if it had been. I make it my business never to regress anything."

Dorothy shuddered and made a choking noise, turning away from this wanton talk. She said, "What's your take on this, Sue?"

Sue shrugged her shoulders. "Well, I was never very bothered about sex. I could take it or leave it, quite frankly. But it's interesting to ponder what Bella and Gussie did. It's the way of the world, isn't it."

"But do you approve? You must have a view."

Sue's face was blank. "No, well, yes, I mean, no. Actually, I don't care what people get up to sex-wise. I'm not sure how I feel about blackmail."

"Oh, don't be so naive. You'd let men interfere with little children, or rape women at will?"

"Of course not," Sue said, waving a hand at the letters and cards, "but these men are consenting adults."

With her head held high, Dorothy gave them the benefit of her considered opinion that both are unacceptable in a civilised society, but prostitution was the more heinous crime of the two. Rampant sex destroyed lives. Blackmail just made people poor—or poorer, since nobody blackmailed someone who had nothing.

Both Sue and Evie hooted in surprise. Sue said, "So on a scale of one to ten, where would you put prostitution?"

Dorothy didn't have to think. "Ten, of course."

"And blackmail?"

"I suppose I would rate it nine, but that doesn't mean I approve of it,"

"No, but you would agree that these things are often relative. A little money asked from someone who has a lot and wouldn't miss it, for example, is no bad thing, especially if it benefited a needy blackmailer. And if the victim deserved to pay for their misdeeds, like a married man visiting a prostitute, what then?" Sue had found it in herself to be argumentative and smiled as she spoke. Evie sat nearby, nodding her agreement and muttering, "A heinous crime — what does it mean?"

There was a long silence while Dorothy stared at Sue. "Very clever," she said at last. "Who would have guessed it of you. It must have been all that fish we had last night."

Dorothy was not prepared to be persuaded by the logic of Sue's arguments but nevertheless she was unnerved by the force of her words. For the first time, her position in the little group felt diminished. It was unusual to have Sue, or anyone, take control and it made her uncomfortable. To hide her chagrin, and to indicate that she would not engage any further in these unsavoury discussions, she picked up a back copy of *Gardeners' World* and pretended to interest herself in the finer points of compost making. Let the two women rabbit on if they wished.

She was aware that they had inched closer together and were talking in undertones. She kept her eyes glued to the page but she could hear what was said very well. Sue was arguing that blackmailing a small sum was not such a great crime and Evie was agreeing, adding, *"Are you thinking what I'm thinking?"* And Sue replied, *"Probably,"* glancing in Dorothy's direction as she said it.

How annoying it was to see how close those two had become. Two of a kind, but why was that a surprise? She had spent her life trying to be different; not one of the herd, but in this case being sidelined was not welcome. Evie's anxious voice cut into her thoughts. *"But who would we choose if we wanted to have a go? Bella and Gussie had all their clients but we don't know anyone like that."* There was a pause then Sue said, *"We will have to keep our ears open. All I know is how tired I am of being poor."*

At that point, Dorothy had heard enough. It wasn't her fault that they were poor but still a smidgen of guilt had gripped her. She stood up, threw down the magazine and marched from the room.

Evie and Sue looked at each other. Dorothy had made her views abundantly clear.

"We are both tired of being paupers?" Sue continued.

"That is so true," Evie replied, grabbing Sue's arm. "Dotty wants us to throw all these papers away as waste paper but I want to keep them. We may be able to use them sometime."

"Let's put them out of sight, back in the drawer, then."

They piled up the letters, envelopes and postcards and stacked them on top of the desk. The secret drawer was still open. Evie bent to look inside. "It goes a long way back. Did we take everything out?" She reached back as far as she could. "There is something else. We missed this." and she pulled out a small black notebook. "I say, Dorothy doesn't know about this!"

They swiftly packed the papers into the drawer then sat to examine the find. There were neatly written lists, names and addresses, followed by the aliases they recognised, plus many, many more. The last addition on many names was a £ sign with an amount penciled in.

They looked at each other. "This is just what we need," Sue whispered. "It tells us the names of their clients and where they live. Look, some have an added word by their name. Mr Sixpack cheats on his wife, apparently. There are several with *adulterer*, here's one with *rich* and here's another with just *P.* I wonder what P stands for."

"Peedo, predatory, plump, pissed, pig… could be any of those. We will have to keep this from Miss Prudeypants, won't we?"

"Absolutely. I suppose the names without money added means they were clients they didn't think were worth blackmailing. It leaves them wide open for someone to have a go." Sue looked hard at Evie.

"Oh, let's have a go. Go on, let's. Just once. I'm game if you are." Evie was bouncing up and down like an excited child. "There's no reason why the two of us could not do it by ourselves. We never agreed to do everything in threes."

Sue looked a bit doubtful. "If we do, we'll have to plan it carefully and give her no hint. She will kick up an awful fuss if she finds out."

They decided to meet in Sue's bedroom to talk it through, thinking that if they succeeded, it would serve

Dorothy right for being such a killjoy. Later that evening when Dorothy had retired, the two women met to choose someone from the list they thought would be a good subject. They chose a Mr H. Collins, alias Hotlips Harry. He had *adulterer* after his name but no sum of money, and he lived only a few miles down the road. Evie had already chosen the most appropriate of the demand letters, so it only remained to decide a date and time for the drop.

In bed that night, Dorothy could not get the day's discussions out of her mind. She knew that she would never involve herself in anything remotely criminal. She had her principles. As usual, their three opinions fell at each end of the moral spectrum, Evie at one end and herself at the other, with Sue somewhere in between. That was always how it fell in the house; a *yes* versus a *no* with a *maybe* in the middle. She would have to put her foot down and reinstate some ethical tone to the household. She was dealing with adults after all, if you could call Evie an adult.

Evie was also lying in bed, thinking, in her woolly night cap, her pink bedsocks and the electric blanket turned up to high. There was no analysis going on in her mind. She was enjoying a fantasy, making it up as she went along. She was a sex goddess, and men queued up, begging her to chastise them with her little whip. She never hit them very hard which was why they all adored her. She wasn't wearing much, just one of those lacy corset bustier things. The candlelight flattered her thighs that miraculously were now smooth and firm, the reward for all her dancing exercise.

Sue lay in a moral quandary, biting her nails and trying to make up her mind. She and Evie were going ahead and she needed to go over all the likely snags and dangers inherent in the plan to exhort money from Mr Hotlips. Would she be able to go out in the dead of night to deprive this poor chap of his beer money, his football ticket or his wife's birthday present? If she only knew how bad he was, how deserving of his loss, she might find it in her heart to despise him long enough to get the job done.

They needed the cash so very badly for the repairs. It was many years since she had been so poor. Marriage had changed all that. When her husband died, she had to budget a little, but now there was only her old age pension to live on. Taste, style and quality had always been her watchwords and it went against the grain to make do with cheddar instead of camembert or the cheapest asparagus on the supermarket shelves.

Despite all the doubts, in the morning, Sue and Evie enjoyed a new excitement. They double-checked that Mr Hotlips Harry was indeed the right choice of victim. They re-read the letter chosen from the bundle in the drawer.

> *What price peace of mind?*
> *Your secret can be safe with me.*
> *Bring £500 to Derek Robinson R.I.P.*
> *in the cemetery on the left, five rows back*
> *or suffer the consequences.*
> *On 7th of November at midnight.*
> *Signed, a friend.*

"That should do it, but we'll have to change the date," Sue said. "This letter is more than two years old. We'll have to give it at least a week to allow for the post."

The message was retyped and redated. Evie was about to sign her name at the bottom when Sue stopped her just in time. She produced a brown envelope and the letter was popped inside and stamped. She would post it in the morning.

"Are you sure midnight is necessary? One of us will have to go out after midnight to pick up the money and lose our beauty sleep," whispered Sue from the boot room where they were both hiding from Dorothy.

Evie volunteered on the spot. "It's only one night, and you will have to stay up to let me in when I come back with the loot. I love the summer nights, the moonlight, the cry of owls and the smell of the dew. It will be like going to Swan Lake."

"There might be people around any earlier. You don't want to be recognised. You'll have to disguise yourself."

"I do hope it won't be too dark at that time. I'm rather afraid of the dark ever since I found a monster under my bed."

"This is a fine time to tell me. What kind of monster?"

"Well actually it was Bojo, my clown puppet, but until Daddy fished him out I was paralipstick with fear and I have relived that moment ever since."

Sue sighed and shook her head in disbelief. "It is amazing what one's imagination can do. I thought I saw a ghost once but I think it was my husband's spirit come to pay me back for cremating him. He was worried that at the Last Trump, he would have no physical body to rise from the grave and he'd lose his place in the queue at the Pearly Gates."

The cemetery was a fifteen-minute walk away, but they decided Evie should not leave the house until a quarter past midnight, to give Hotlips Harry time to scarper. They supposed he would be unlikely to hang about. Evie would be back by one o'clock at the latest and Sue would pretend to go to bed but stay awake to let her in. In the morning, they would have the pleasure of handing a wad of notes to Dorothy.

Despite their care, Dorothy noticed something was up. She heard the murmur of voices through the bedroom wall and noticed odd disappearances during the day. When asked, both women vigorously denied everything, instantly fortifying her suspicions. She had heard Evie mention "prudeypants" as they whispered together in the hall and she was most put out. She wore a frozen smile for days and watched them both like a hawk. They were supposed to be a team and it wasn't fair to cut her out of their plans. Perhaps it was because she held different opinions and expressed them too forcibly. She had never cared what people thought because she was usually right, but somehow this time she did care and was hurt.

On the day, Evie claimed she was feeling dizzy and went to bed in the afternoon for a long nap. She wanted to be alert for the night's adventure when nervous energy and courage would be required. Sue wanted to do the same but reckoned it would give the game away, hoping that maybe she could doze during her long wait.

They both pretended to go to bed but put on more clothes instead of taking them off. At midnight they each crept down the hall where Sue questioned Evie.

"Have you got a torch? Have you got better shoes on than your usual ballet pumps? Have you got a bag to put the money in and where's your hat to hide your face if you meet anyone?" Finally she asked, "Do you know the way to the cemetery?"

"Of course I do. That's where they put Daddy."

With that, Sue let Evie out into the night.

Nine

It was chilly at that time of night and Evie shivered as she walked down the Close to the main road. The sky was cloudy but in the gaps between the clouds, she could see the stars, and moonlight broke fitfully through. Most of the houses were dark with the odd lighted window here and there. Soon she came to the cemetery gates with the dark edifice of the church looming beyond. Luckily, the gates were not locked, and they creaked and squealed as she passed through. *Now then*, she thought, *where is that tomb?* It was the grave of... goodness, she couldn't remember the man's name or where he could be found. She did remember the RIP but soon discovered they all had that. Why hadn't she written it down, knowing how bad her memory was these days?

All she could think of to do was to wander up and down between the gravestones looking for a parcel or a package left for her to collect. In the moonlight, all the gravestones looked like crooked giant teeth. It was a large area and it took some time. Any feelings of urgency she'd had evaporated over ten minutes or so, and to entertain herself she remembered a piece of music by Saint-Saëns about the devil playing his fiddle in the graveyard to arouse the dead, who rose from their graves. They danced all night until the cock crowed and dawn broke, and in an instant they sank back into the earth. *Danse Macabre,* it was called, and she felt inspired to dance there and then as she imagined the skeletons might. She capered, she spun, she waved her arms, imagining the rattle of her bones. When she stopped and stood in the silence she heard an amused guffaw from someone behind her. Whirling round, she saw a tramp sitting on the grass, leaning his back against one of the stones, laughing at her.

"Funny time to have a cabaret," he said in a gravelly voice. There was an empty bottle and a burger wrapper on the ground beside him.

"Funny place to have a picnic," she retorted.

"Needs must. I ain't got no home to go to."

"Is this the best you could find?"

"I like bein outdoors in the night. It's special, with no folk around, and with only little wild things for company. You's a little wild thing, ain't yer. What you doin here, anyway?"

"I came to pick something up. You haven't seen anything left on a tomb, have you? Cos if you have, it's mine."

"Now that would be tellin, wouldn't it?"

Evie sagged a little, and sighing, plumped herself down on the grass and yawned. "It's past my bedtime," she muttered.

"All that dancin took it out of yer, did it? Nice though. As good as the telly. Is you famous or summat?"

"I had dreams of being famous. I could have been. It's in my blood. Margot, Alicia, Anna, Darcey, they are my heroes."

"Oh ay, never heard of them."

"Dreams was all I had. My Daddy said I wasn't strong enough, so my ambition was wasted. You know you're leaning on my Daddy's grave, don't you."

"I said hello to him when I come."

"Aren't you frightened of ghosts or zombies, sitting here all by yourself?"

"Nah, why does everyone think that good people turn into scary killers just as soon as they're in the ground? Look around, mums and dads, sisters and lil bairns, who'd be scared of them?"

They chatted on and Evie learned that his name was Wilf and he was a homeless wanderer. She told him something of herself, where she lived and about having no money.

"I ain't got no money neither, but I manage well enough. You should join me in my wanderin"

"Can't. Got to find this package." And she leaped up, remembering her mission. "I'm in really big trouble if I can't find it. My partner is waiting for me."

"He's a bad'un, is he?'

"Oh no, he's a woman," and she skipped off.

"Nice to meet yer," she heard him call as she went.

When she got back she found Sue fast asleep on the sofa. She tip-toed upstairs to bed, leaving explanations until the morning.

Sue woke with a start. Sunlight was shining through the crack in the curtains. Dorothy stood, arms akimbo, looking down at her ."What on earth are you doing down here? Haven't you been to bed?"

Sue sat up and rubbed her eyes. Yawning, giving herself time to think, she pulled her brain into gear. "I had a good reason. What time is it? Where's Evie?"

"In bed, I assume, where I expected you to be. What good reason?"

Squinting about the room in case Evie had left a package when she had returned in the early hours, and seeing nothing, Sue decided to tell all. There was no point in hiding the facts; they would have to own up sooner or later. "Evie went out last night to pick up the blackmail money."

Dorothy's eyes opened wide. "The what? What have you two done behind my back? I knew something was going on."

"We sent one of the letters demanding £500. Evie went out last night to fetch it."

They had never heard Dorothy screech before but she screeched now. "You idiots, you've turned yourselves into criminals overnight! What fools you are going to look when you discover that man has gone to the police. Are you sure she's in her bed? The police were probably waiting for her and have taken her to the cop shop. They will search you out and hunt you both down. What is that going to look like in the local press?"

Sue struggled to stand up before the incandescent Dorothy and immediately regressed to her pre-assertive self. "Oh dear, do you really think so? We were very careful."

Sue then told her the ins and outs of their scheme while Dorothy listened, her face registering disbelief. After hearing all, she finally said, "And not a word to me! I can't get over it."

"Well, we knew you'd never agree."

"So you went ahead despite my views."

Sue looked at the floor. "Evie thought we should try it just once."

"Oh, she did, did she? As I recall you were equally keen. So, where is this £500 you both went to so much trouble to get?"

"I expect Evie's got it."

Evie, of course, had overslept. Her overnight jaunt had taken its toll on her energy levels but she had danced in her dream with a raggedy old tramp with the face of Rudolf Nureyev and she didn't want it to stop. When she finally did appear she was met by a subdued Sue and a hopping mad Dorothy, who launched straight into her attack. "I hear you and Sue here have been depriving some poor soul out of a quantity of cash. And at eighty, walking the streets at midnight in pursuit of your ill-gotten gains, well, I would have expected you to be more sensible. I've a good mind to make you give the money back. It is tainted money, dirty money, and you are the one who initiated the plan. It will serve you right when the police come to the door. Don't expect me to defend you, you stupid booby."

Evie stood listening to this tirade of abuse, odd emotions coming and going over her face. "Why are you making such a fuss? We haven't robbed a bank or murdered anyone," she said at last. "If I want to walk at night, I shall. As for money, there isn't any. I looked everywhere but couldn't find any envelope or package.

So there! Now, you can get off your sanctimonious high horse."

That took the wind out of Dorothy's sails and she paused, stepped back and unclenched her fists. "Huh," she said at last. "Then what a waste of time. Thankfully no harm done, but next time you and Sue decide to act alone, I hope you'll choose something less risky." Looking somewhat flushed, she turned and left the room.

Sue hissed at Evie when Dorothy was out of earshot, "I knew she'd be cross. What happened?"

"It was like I said. There was no package on any grave."

"I waited a long time. What kept you?"

"I was searching, wasn't I." She didn't bother to mention Wilf and her chat with him. "And before you say anything more, I'm cross too. She called me a booby and that is just too rude, too unpleasant to bear and I've had enough of her talking to me as if I was an idiot child."

Eager to reassure Evie, Sue said, "She'll get over it. We did try, didn't we? Come and have some breakfast."

"No, I won't get over it. And I can't bear to stay in the same room with her, so I'm going out and I don't know when I'll be back."

With these words, she turned, tripped over the rug, executed a dance step never seen before, and stumbled to the front door.

From the kitchen, Sue and Dorothy heard the front door slam. A stony-faced Dorothy was scrambling an egg with unnecessary vigour and Sue was "pardoning and sorrying" around her as she made the coffee. A few minutes later they heard the door open and Evie stood in the doorway with a package in her hands.

"I found this on the step and before you ask, I have no idea who left it. It looks as if it's been opened and half the money has gone."

"Really? How nice when they could have taken it all. £250 is better than none, I suppose," said Sue.

Dorothy paused in her scrambling, anger and suspicion written over her face. "How did they know where to come? Were you followed on the way home? Don't tell me you put our address on the letter. That would be just like you."

Evie looked daggers at Dorothy but said nothing. She walked forward to hand the money to her.

"Don't give it to me. I want no part in this nonsense," Dorothy said, turning away from her, so Evie went to the desk and put the notes inside the drawer marked *Savings* then walked out. They heard the door slam for a second time.

"Where's she going?"

Sue fished a teabag out of her mug and took it dripping to the bin. "I have no idea," she said.

Ten

Evie might have hopped, skipped and jumped down the Close as usual but not today. She was wounded. Nobody said nasty things to her usually and if they did, she didn't listen. Dorothy was a cow. If only Daddy was still around; he would have made mincemeat of her. He would have told her where to get off in no uncertain terms.

It must have been Wilf who had left the package on the step for she had told him where she lived. She remembered exaggerating the trouble she was in. She had called her partner a monstrous termagant because she rather liked the word. He must have thought that was some kind of dangerous insect. How nice of him to be so helpful! There were some good people left in the world, thank goodness.

It wasn't long before her happy nature reasserted itself – either that, or the limitations of her 80-year-old memory did the trick. What did she care about bossy Dorothy and her nasty ways? She wasn't going to spend any time in her company if she could help it.

Wilf was a nice man and had probably found the package before she had arrived at the cemetery. She wasn't going to blame him for taking half of the money; he was worse off than they were. Perhaps he could use it to rent a room. That would be good. He might have taken all of it but instead, he had thought of her and her trouble. That was nice, wasn't it?

And she gave a little skip and went on her way.

Back at Eyesore Towers, the day drew on. After a sullen lunch when Evie had still not returned, both Sue and Dorothy began to fidget.

"I hope nothing has happened to her. Do you think she might have fallen over?" Sue said.

Dorothy shrugged. She was beginning to think she had been a bit harsh with Evie. She had talked as if she was chastising one of her girls and that wasn't appropriate. She must learn to hold her tongue. Evie was a child but there were bits of her mature enough to resent such scolding. She wandered aimlessly about the house, not knowing what to focus on until she knew Evie was safe. Was there a book on how to be un-assertive opposite the one Sue had read? She resolved to try harder to be more understanding. Evie pleased and annoyed her in equal measure but she must concentrate on being pleased in the future. It would be hard, but she would try.

Sue had been thinking about how they might spend the £250. Some would go to Odd Bob for his last bill. The rest could go on the kitchen cabinets, on the doors hanging loose on their hinges, or the loose banister that was surely a health hazard. Perhaps some draught excluder. There wouldn't be enough to fix the roof leaks or the showers. Fortunately the boiler was sorted but some of the radiators leaked and maybe they could be done.

She looked out of the window at the massing clouds. Rain was forecast. Evie had gone out without her coat and a soaking would chill her to the bone and possibly kill her. If anything, she was more worried than Dorothy. Evie had talked as if she wanted to leave the house and perhaps that was what she had done. She was just cute enough to throw herself on the mercy of some understanding housing executive with a tale of being homeless and penniless. Or she might have been taken in by some sympathetic do-gooder. What would they do if she didn't come back? How she would miss Evie, always cheerful and enthusiastic about everything! She cooked bizarre food and wore clothes appropriate for a teenager but she was fun to have around. Sue didn't fancy the future with only Dorothy as a companion.

By tea time there was still no sign of Evie. Curiosity had given way to concern and now they were both seriously anxious, reminding themselves that Evie was over eighty and though she tried hard to convince people she was younger, there was no denying the years. What could have happened? She had nowhere else to go. Should they ring the hospital? Had she suffered a memory lapse and forgotten the way home or got on a bus and forgotten to get off? Had she been arrested? Now that was a terrible thought.

At seven o'clock, Evie walked in. They both rushed to her, eager to know where she had been but Evie was tight-lipped. When offered supper, she blithely refused.

"I had lunch and a good tea, so all I want is a cup of tea with oat milk. I think I'm going to become a vegan," she declared, ignoring all questions about her absence. It did not satisfy as an explanation but it was all they got.

While the clouds in the sky grew and blackened, the clouds in the house lightened with her return.

"It looks as if you were back just in time," Sue observed as she watched the evening weather forecast on the television.

"No matter, I shall sleep like a log; I've had such a busy day, so it can rain all it likes. In fact, I think I'll go to bed now. Goodnight both," and Evie made for the stairs.

The storm broke in the night. The lightening woke Dorothy and she got up to check the leak bucket was not overflowing but then slept through the crash, as did Sue and Evie. The next morning, they awoke to a clean sunny world and only slowly noticed the damage the storm had wrought. A tree had blown down and fallen against the back of the house, breaking windows and forcing branches into the downstairs rooms. The roof had given up several more tiles and a small flood had seeped under the kitchen door, forming a pond two inches deep. The roof of the conservatory had caved in and broken glass lay everywhere.

With so many holes in the fabric, the house was cold and the three women shivered as they surveyed the devastation.

Dorothy was dumbstruck by the extremity of the damage. The disaster was so severe, if anyone had planned it, they couldn't have done more to threaten their livelihood or their wellbeing. So much for peace and harmony, she thought. What was their future to be now?

Sue had clasped her hands and, despairing, sank to the floor. She looked up at Dorothy. "This is the end, isn't it? We will never, ever be able to fix all this," but there was nothing Dorothy could find to say to her.

Evie got over the shock more quickly than the others and put her hand over her mouth to hide her amusement. This event was so ultra catastrophic, so extreme, it was almost funny. She surveyed the rubble around her, considered for a moment, then decided to be positive. "This is an insurance job. Surely that will cover it."

Dorothy growled. "Insurance, are you kidding? We haven't got any insurance. It was an added expense, if you remember. It was another £400 we hadn't got."

Evie's face sobered at once. "But isn't it illegal? Like running a car uninsured?"

"No, I checked at the time. I thought we would get it later when we were more solvent. I thought it unlikely the house would fall down any time soon." She gave a hollow mirthless laugh. "Of course, this is the next best thing."

The sight of the mess was so depressing, they decided to sit in the kitchen. Nobody could think of anything useful to say so a gloomy silence prevailed. After several minutes, Evie, doing her best to look on the bright side said she had an idea.

All eyes turned in her direction.

"Has anyone got life insurance? If one of us was to die, life insurance would cover it," she said.

Dorothy gave her a disgusted stare.. "You are absolutely crackers, Evie. Would you be willing to volunteer to see that through?"

Suppressing a giggle, Evie said. "I was just brainstorming. You are supposed to say anything that comes into your head when you brainstorm."

Dorothy waved her hand impatiently. "Oh, stop being so ridiculous. This is a serious matter. We may have to move out and it will be the Care Home for all of us. Just what we dreaded." There were groans all round.

With nothing to hold on to, Sue struggled to stand. "I am going to have hysterics. I can feel it coming on. And in case you ask, I haven't got life insurance."

They made a list of everything that needed doing and added it to the list compiled before the storm. There was no point in trying to cost all the items for the work would need a fortune and there was only £5.70p in the savings drawer, along with the £250 Evie had put in. At least that much would allow them to eat while they did what they could to clear up the mess.

They mopped the kitchen floor and packed the bottom of the door with woollen scarves. They cut all the invading branches and nailed boards found in the shed over the window openings. They swept up the glass on the floor of the conservatory and renamed it the Sun Room. They acquired three more buckets for the extra roof leaks and made notes on all the new damp patches. It was sad work and they went about it silently as no sensible solution had been suggested, and talking about it made them all feel worse. Their glum faces matched the gloom outside.

The weather was dreary, they were dreary. Unable to afford to go anywhere, they turned to their hobbies to fill the hours. Sue, to everyone's relief, abandoned *The Lark Ascending* and attempted to cheer herself up with some old traditional songs like *Knees Up Mother Brown* and *Ten Green Bottles*. Her attempts penetrated from the shed and through the broken windows, to the puzzlement of Evie and Dorothy, who could not tell one tune from the other.

Dorothy wandered about like a lost soul, refusing offers of card games, jigsaws or quizzes. "Why are we wasting time? We should be doing something. Isn't there ANYTHING you can think of?"

She was answered by shaken heads and silence. Odd Job Bob never worked at the weekend and even if he did, the work would overwhelm him and his bill would be enormous. So they carried on, doing the best they could with the devastation all around them.

"What are you reading while we do all the work?" She asked Evie pointedly. "Is that *Anne of Green Gables* for the fourth time?" Evie merely stared at her as if she hadn't heard, no doubt lost in a fantasy world all of her own.

It took another week before the weather improved. Sue went outside to see how things were in the garden. The tree still leaned against the house wall. The shed was a little more worse for wear but would survive. On her way back into the house she looked up at the facade and noticed that another window on the first floor was broken. They hadn't noticed it, as the room that the window served was the locked room. She stood looking up and decided the glass would have to be replaced, but that would give someone the opportunity to climb into that room and unlock it from inside. If only they had a ladder. Odd Job Bob had a ladder. Perhaps he could do it.

Eleven

Cursing his ill-luck because he hated climbing ladders, but unable to say no, Bob did as he was asked. He was immensely fond of his grandmother, and these three old dears put him in mind of her. He was sorry for their incompetence, and amused by their grandiose plans for this wreck they had bought. They did pay their bills, which was a blessing, though they were mostly late. If he stopped doing odd jobs for them he reckoned he would not see payment at all.

He climbed his ladder, gingerly inching his way through the branches of the tree. At the top he picked out the broken glass and peered into the interior of the room, then turned to call down to the women waiting below. "Looks like some kind of store room." Then with great caution he manoeuvred himself into the room and went straight to the door. They wanted it opened and that he could do. Down below he heard the tall one say, "Full of useless junk, I've no doubt." And then the soppy one said, "It's a good job Bob's going up. I would be putrified if it were me."

It meant breaking the lock, which he did, then he went to the window and gave thumbs up to the three waiting down below. The room was gloomy and seemed to be full of dark stuff and metal things that glinted in the light. None of his business, so he nailed a board to the gap, making the room quite dark, and left by the newly opened door.

They had all trooped up to the landing, waiting eagerly for news of what was in the room. Bob shook his head. "There's summat in there, a lot of stuff but I didn't look. I'll leave you ladies to get on with your exploring." He was heartily glad he didn't have to get down that ladder and mentally added a substantial amount of danger money to the bill.

The three of them stood inside the room and looked around, until their eyes had become accustomed to the gloom. What they saw stunned them. There were cardboard boxes, piles of footwear in one corner, metal items they couldn't identify hanging from hooks on the walls, and a rack full of what looked like clothes or costumes. They wandered around; everything was black or red and the smell of mouldering leather was dreadful. Evie made for the clothes. A nurse's costume, a maid's uniform and one or two others were first but then there were corsets and bustiers, bikinis made of vinyl, a latex cat suit and a variety of body suits in black leather, all with chains and zips, straps here and there and lacy inserts, metal rings and buckles.

Evie smiled to herself and clapped her hands. "You know what all this is, don't you? It's Bella and Gussie's stock room."

Sue and Dorothy had been wandering around, perplexed by what they found. "Tell us what it is then, Miss Clever Clogs." Sue said.

Dorothy interrupted. "Do prostitutes need all this stuff?"

They had been picking up items they could not identify and many they did, like the whips and the canes, the dog collars with leads attached.

Evie said, "This stuff was part of it. They had to leave it all behind. I wonder if they will want it back."

Sue opened a chest of drawers and found some face masks and hoods. She tried an elaborate cat's eye mask and turning to the others said, "How about this then?" Then she began sorting through a variety of whips, wearing black vinyl gloves that reached almost to her armpits. She picked out a whip with multiple thongs and with a flick of her wrist cracked it close to Dorothy's legs.

Dorothy flinched. "Careful, if you are going to be assertive with that, keep away from me."

"I was thinking it was just the thing to keep you in order, no more of your nasty cracks or you'll get a crack from this!"And with another deft flick, the whip skimmed dangerously close to Dorothy's bottom.

"I would LOVE to wear this," said Evie from the far side of the room, holding up a skimpy body suit.

"Now is your chance," muttered Dorothy, picking up a hood with finger and thumb, holding it at arm's length. "What's the use of a hood with no eye holes? It's like wearing a paper bag and it smells atrocious."

Sue looked over at Evie, who was intent on holding the body suit up against herself. There was so little of it, more flesh would be on display than was covered. She said, "Aren't they cold with all that bare skin on show? Goose pimples are not very sexy, nor is being blue."

"They probably claimed they were shivering with passion," Dorothy said dryly, turning her attention to the collars.

Sue, thoroughly mystified by what she was seeing, said, "I didn't know prostitutes used all this gear. I thought they just let men do it and then took the money."

Evie had moved on to a number of paddles next to the canes. "These are what they spank with," and she waved one as if it was a bat. "It would be good for ping pong, don't you think? Do we have any balls to play with?"

"I expect we could find you some if you are determined. There are plenty of balls out there." Sue indicated the outdoors.

Dorothy turned to her. "We'll have less of the filthy jokes, if you don't mind."

Evie said, "It must be good exercise, all that spanking. Not so good for the arthritis but I bet they end up with a strong right arm."

"But when do they do that, before or after the sex?" Sue was frowning as she held up a rubber mask.

"No, no, you've got it all wrong." Evie grinned at them. "These women were not prostitutes."

"What were they then, and how come you know so much about it?" Sue asked.

"They were sex workers. I had a friend who was a domme when I was young. She told me all about it."

"What is a domme?" they chorused.

"It's short for dominatrix. You know, sado-masochism, bondage and all that caper?"

Mystified, they shook their heads. Dorothy said, "Well yes, we've heard of it but that's all. If that is a sex worker, there must be sex involved."

"It is a domme's job to inflict pain on those men, or women, who enjoy being hurt, or like submitting to someone. It makes the clients feel sexy, but not the domme. They are not supposed to have sex. They just

118

dole out the punishment and the clients pay for the privilege. My friend said she just used to shout abuse at them and make them bow down to her. She used to tie them up then slap them. She put nappies on some men and scolded them until they cried, then cuddled them and gave them a baby's bottle."

"Well I never. And they got paid good money for that?"

"Oh yes, my friend did very well."

Sue and Dorothy looked around them with new eyes.

Dorothy glowered. "I did hear something of this sort of activity some years ago but I shut my mind to it straight away, you may be sure." She was holding up a thong with several balls at intervals.

Sue shook her head. "I am such an innocent. This is all news to me. I've never heard of a domme."

Evie said, "Well, now you have, and this is the stuff they use."

Sue's imagination was in overdrive. She picked up one of the cat suits. "No wonder this place smells. Think of all the sweating. Wearing rubber makes for a terrible amount of sweating. Can you imagine it, leaking out all over the place?" She shuddered but then laughed as she, pushed her feet into a pair of long boots with immensely high heels. She then fixed a thick leather collar with a metal buckle round her neck but stumbled as she took a step towards the mirror to see how it suited her. "Not used to heels," she grinned, hanging on to a metal bar. "Hilarious. Don't I look a treat? You would have to be young to wear all this."

There were many more things to investigate but Dorothy had seen enough. "I feel assaulted," she said. "How about a cup of tea and leave the rest for another time." She led the way downstairs with Sue and Evie giggling along behind her.

Those two agreed that it had been the most entertaining afternoon they had spent in a long time but Dorothy would concede only that it was 'interesting'.

"You never did this yourself, did you, Evie? Were you not tempted to follow suit?" Sue said.

"Oh no, Daddy wouldn't like it. He didn't like me consorting with other men." When she had gone to use the facilities, Sue and Dorothy were thoughtful.

"I bet that's why she never married. Daddy wouldn't allow it," Sue examined her nails while she thought about this. "Was he a nice man, this Daddy?"

Dorothy shook her head. "I never met him so I don't know. They were obviously very close though."

"Mm, I wonder just how close," Sue replied. The goings on in the locked room had brought to mind thoughts of other unsavoury activities she had heard about on the television.

Twenty minutes later Evie reappeared. She stood in the doorway and said, "How do you like this, then?"

They gasped when they saw her. She was striking a pose, smiling coyly over her shoulder. The sight took their breath away for she was wearing one of the elaborate corsets, the one decorated with roses and red hearts. With it were the tiniest of lacy briefs and fishnet stockings, garters and the highest of the high-heeled shoes. The bra was the red vinyl one and she had elbow length gloves, the very shiny sort that were as stiff as a metal gauntlet.

Dorothy gaped, then said, "What DO you look like?"

"Don't you think I look the part?" Evie grinned and staggered forward and they had a better view of her. The stockings did not hide her varicose veins or her less-than-smooth thighs. The red bra resembled two deflated balloons. Her neck, no longer disguised by her usual clothes, was now revealed as… well there was no other word but scrawny. Below, her shoulder blades stuck out like clothes hangers.

Sue, not wishing to hurt Evie's feelings, bared her teeth in an attempt at a smile. "Were you thinking of going to a fancy dress party, dear?"

"If I was, I'd go as a domme."

Dorothy was shaking her head sadly. "I am no expert but to me you don't look very sexy." *Grotesque* was what she was thinking.

"Oh, really? Well, it is just a bit of fun," Evie said, as she tried to revolve on the spot, hampered somewhat by the spiky high heels but finally giving them a view of lace covered buttocks, that, like everything else, failed to charm.

"For goodness sake, take it all off – you look terrible!" Dorothy blurted out.

Thinking about what Bella and Gussie had done with all that gear made their talk unusually animated. After arguments, surprise and excitement, they finally decided that however bizarre and unacceptable to decent people it all was, and apart from ministering to people's perversions, there really was no harm in it. Even Dorothy surprised them by saying, "Well, at least it isn't blackmail."

"So you are not dead against it then?" Sue ventured.

."I really don't care what adults get up to as long as it is not cruel or illegal or likely to corrupt the young, but it is certainly not how I would want to spend my time."

Evie said, "Oh, I would have thought you might enjoy it, knowing how you feel about men. Wouldn't you like to give some men a good whipping?"

"Are you suggesting that I don't like men?" Dorothy sat up, indignation oozing from every pore.

"But you don't, do you? You've said so yourself many times. You are snotty to Odd Job Bob. He can do nothing right. You complain volubly about how men run the world. And I know you like telling people what you think, no matter how hurtful that is. That is a way of inflicting pain, mental pain, and I should know."

"You are making me out to be a sadist." Dorothy looked around at their faces.

Sue was shaking her head. In retreat as usual, she said, "Oh no, we wouldn't go that far."

"I would," Evie admitted. "You aren't very careful of other people's feelings."

"That is a long way from proving I am a sadist. Are there any more insulting things you are going to throw at me because if there is I'm going to my room."

Evie said, "Don't take it personally, dear. I was joking," as she made this half-hearted apology, but the muttered "if the cap fits!" under her breath.

In the silence that then reigned, the phone rang. Sue answered it and came back to tell them that Mavis wanted to know when they would be returning to her *Dancing for Grandmothers* class.

Glumly, Dorothy said, "We can't go back. We can't afford the coffee, or the bus fare. They will all be there wanting to know about our move. What are we going to tell them; that it was a failure? That we are stony-broke and living in a house that is crumbling about our ears? No, I couldn't face them."

Sue said, "One of my teeth fell out yesterday and I'd hate to be seen with this awful gap. I can't afford to go to the dentist so I propose to stay indoors. I told Mavis we would get back to her."

"Have you tried superglue, Sue?" Evie said. "I knew a trombonist once who used that because he had wrecked his embouthingy when a front tooth fell out."

"Fortunately, a missing tooth won't affect my violin playing."

"We will have to do something. Couldn't one of you get a job? I'll answer some adverts, if you like," Evie said.

"At our age? Not a hope. People expect us to volunteer."

"Couldn't we do what Bella and Gussie did?" This was Evie again, "They made money and we have all the gear upstairs. We wouldn't have to go anywhere."

There was a chorus of, "Oh no, we couldn't. We wouldn't know what to do."

"Then let ME have a go. I'll do what my friend Jeannie used to do. We could charge £30 for half an hour's spanking. Maybe £50 for a good whipping. What do you say. We are desperate, after all."

Dorothy's face clouded over and Sue leaned over and touched Evie's arm. "You are much too nice to be a domme. Could you make a man go down and lick your feet without giggling? Don't you have to be dominating, powerful and imperious? Sex play is a serious business, I imagine – at least I think it is for the men."

Evie held her head on one side as she thought. "I think you're right. Dorothy would make a far better domme than I would. I don't think I could be hard enough."

Dorothy crossed her arms and tossed her head. "Oh no, a thousand times no. You are not going to push me into that." She shook her head vigorously as she pushed back her chair and stood utterly appalled by the ludicrous suggestion. Determination was written large in her set jaw.

The next day, a bill for removal of the tree arrived. Two men with chain saws for half a day and removal of the logs came to £1200.

Dorothy came into the kitchen at coffee time and told them she had reluctantly changed her mind. She would do it.

Twelve

Although none of them really knew what they would have to do, the project was going to be planned carefully. Dorothy did not want a fiasco like the blackmail attempt. She would take charge and veto any suggestion she did not like, which led to many heated discussions. Evie considered herself to be the expert, which was pushing it, since all she had was her own interpretation of the "facts" her friend Jeannie had told her at least forty-five years earlier.

"These things don't change," she declared, as her imagination blossomed.

But Dorothy had her own ideas. If she had to force herself to do this nonsense, she was going to do it her way. "If you think I'm going to dress up in all that fancy clobber, then you are mistaken," she said.

"Oh, but you must. You won't look authentic," they chorused.

Dorothy groaned. "Remember, I want to try one first. Evie can tell me all she knows."

Evie sat up. "To begin with, you ask them what they like or what they want you to do. You can refuse anything you don't fancy doing. Sometimes it's not a lot they want. Just remember they are all masochists and you need to send them home happy. If you are good, maybe they will send you letters like the ones in the desk."

"Sounds easy enough, but how do we find a customer? One client at £30 is not going to help us get out of this hole."

Sue said, "We must think of it as a business, build it up slowly and advertise our service."

"Aren't you getting carried away," Dorothy said. "We can't advertise, not like they used to.We used to see them pasted in telephone boxes."

"But we have the book. Let's send out a flyer, something anonymous but obvious to a potential client. Something like – *Are you happy? Our trained personnel are ready to help. Ring for a quote. Telephone number blah blah blah. Power, strength and pleasure are our watchwords.*"

Sue patted Evie's shoulder."Oh, that is good. Pleasure is a bit obvious, though. How about *satisfaction* or *enjoyment.* And we could add *Former clients welcome.* That should bring them in."

"Hold on. For God's sake don't send out flyers until I've done one." Dorothy was anxious, thinking she might have to cope with a deluge of clients while her expertise was still zero.

"Okay, agreed. But don't worry, for I have a feeling you are going to be a natural. Now, who is going to pick the first one?" Sue asked.

The flyer was designed and the letter written and sent. They chose a man called Godfrey who called himself *Grateful God* which they all thought had a promising ring. Dorothy felt she could not cope with a macho, six-pack, athletic kind of fellow and fervently hoped he was small and weedy.

The day of the first appointment arrived. Dorothy put on clean M&S underwear, a blouse and her shortest skirt but when she showed herself, there was a protest from Evie. "That won't do. Show me your pants. Oh dear, they are not glamorous enough. They are like something out of a 1930s old women's underwear catalogue."

"But I *am* an old woman."

"Yes, but you have to pay homage to your client's fantasy life. You must titillate them, Dorothy, titillate them."

Hardly knowing the meaning of the word, Dorothy said, "And how do I do that?"

"You must pick something from the room upstairs," Evie cried, and they all three trouped up to supervise the dressing. Evie rifled through the costumes and finally pulled out an all-over body suit in black vinyl. "Put this on."

Horrified, Dorothy eyed it and shook her head. "I am not wearing that. Look, there is no back to it. I'll have a bare bum."

"Exactly, just the thing. Don't you agree, Sue?"

"Don't ask me. You are the expert," Sue replied, turning away to hide a horrified smirk.

"Put on these lacy bikini bottoms first, if you really don't fancy showing a bit of flesh."

"No way. I'll stick with M&S if you don't mind."

"Oh well, if you must. Just don't turn your back on him. How about this cat's mask? It will hide your wrinkles."

Dorothy put on the mask then complained that she couldn't see properly. "I want one with bigger holes and that doesn't smell like a ferret's backside." She tried on a few, and eventually was satisfied with a whole face mask.

Evie was on a roll. "How about some jewellery? These chains would do, round your waist and clamped to each nipple. Just remember not to lift your arms suddenly. We don't want you doing yourself a mischief. Now, these dangly earrings, I think. Wow, that's fantastic. The thigh boots will hide some of your

M&S knickers. Just the little black gloves and we're done." Evie turned to Sue. "What do you think?"

Sue appraised the apparition standing before her. It was a case of howling with laughter or attempting a show of sober, insincere appreciation. She nodded and screwed her face into a serious frown. "I must say, you look the part, Dorothy."

Evie stood back to admire her handiwork. "All you need now is an exotic name. How about Madame Dolores?"

Unused to being submissive, Dorothy groaned and complained. She felt a fool, a scarecrow, a grotesque spectacle, but it had to be borne for she had promised. Even when Evie advanced on her, lipstick in hand, she stood as her thin lips were redrawn in a cupid"s bow. "No need for rouge. I shall be quite flushed enough with embarrassment," she managed to say.

It turned out that Godfrey, or Mr Grateful, as they had decided to call him, when he finally turned up, was gentle and pleasantly vague. There was no written reply to the letter they had sent but on the Friday afternoon there was a ring at the front door and standing on the step was a small fellow with thick-lensed horn-rimmed spectacles and hair thinly plastered over his shiny scalp. Sue acted as receptionist and let him in.

Both Dorothy and he took a step back when they saw each other. She surmised he was expecting either Belladonna or Gussie, and she wasn't expecting anyone so ordinary and so insignificant, nothing like her idea of an adulterer.

He stuttered as he spoke. "I was l-l-looking for the l-lady who lives in this house, an Italian l-l-lady."

Bereft of the power of speech for a long moment, Dorothy swallowed but then blurted out, "Come in. You must be Mr Grateful God. I am Madame Dolores. You have come to the right place but the business has changed hands. The other two women have gone and we ladies have taken over."

"Is.. is it the same business?"

"Oh yes, my companions and I are ready to provide all you should want by way of pleasure. I imagine that is what you are after." With a dramatic sweep of her hand, Madame Dolores opened the door, inviting him further into the hall. He gave a relieved sigh as he followed her to the boot room.

The boot room, just to the left of the front door, had been cleared and prepared for the appointment. Sue had painted the walls red, and Odd Job Bob, although somewhat mystified, had fitted hooks and shelves, and had moved the cabinet with its many drawers down from the once locked room. Some of the gear most likely to be used had been installed about the room and gauzy red headscarves covered the lamps, giving the room a womb-like atmosphere.

Earlier, Evie had phoned the storage company from whom they had acquired the desk, and asked the receptionist if the stuff in their bay had yet been cleared. The woman confirmed that it had. "What were you looking for?"

"I was hoping to find a padded chair or an old sofa and maybe a rug or two."

"No problem," the woman said, "We have several pieces people have discarded, the big heavy stuff mostly. You could come and take your pick. You can take what you want for a nominal sum."

Evie had lashed out on a van and that was how the boot room now sported a scarlet *chaise longue* with a missing leg and a fluffy rug big enough to cover most of the floor space, and all for a tenner.

As Dorothy closed the door, she thought, *Okay, here goes. What shall I do now? What disgusting things does this feeble little chap want me to do?* She was feeling desperately nervous. The man himself was looking wary, even more than a little nervous too. It occurred to her that neither of them looked in control

133

of the situation. Powerful and domineering, Evie had said, but if she didn't buck up, this appointment was going to be an embarrassing failure. It was bad enough having to stand in front of him in these ridiculous garments.

As she removed her dressing gown, she cleared her throat and said to Godfrey, "You can hang your jacket on the back of the door, if you like."

Then she reproached herself for being so feeble. She should have commanded him to hang up his jacket instead of that pathetic invitation. *Time to take control,* she told herself as she struck up an aggressive pose. She turned to Godfrey, and in a loud voice told him to take his clothes off. He stared at her for a moment, bemused by the sight of her, but seemed reluctant to oblige. Telling herself to do better, she took a deep breath and declared, "Today, I am Sergeant Major Forbes, and you do as I say or it will be the worse for you. Now, who am I?"

Godfrey took off his glasses and stuffed them in his trouser pocket. The sight of her was obviously too diverting and the shortest of short sight was preferable.

"You are S-S-Sergeant M-M-Major F-Forbes."

"Say it properly. If you can't, I'll have to punish you."

He squinted quickly up at her. "Oh yes, please do. Shall I lie down?"

"Yes, lie down at once," Dorothy ordered, and then watched him lie spreadeagled face down on the rug. "I'm going to give you a good spanking. That's what you need."

"Oh I do, I do."

"But leave your shorts on."

" I p-prefer to put my own knickers on, if you d-don't m-mind."

"What?"

"I usually w-wear my own, if it's all the s-same to you."

"Where are these… knickers?"

"In my j-jacket pocket."

Dorothy went to his jacket and from one of the pockets, brought out a pair of lacy nylon women's knickers, very pretty but minimal in size.

"Put them on," she ordered, making a mental note to mug up on knicker fetishes. When he was again flat on the rug, she took the biggest paddle, and gave him a timorous experimental tap on his nylon covered bottom. He didn't move or make a sound. "That's for starters, the next will be harder."

There was a muffled reply that sounded like eager submission to the inevitable, so she set to with a will.

Slowly his cheeks took on a rose tint, then a ruby glow and then a striking maroon. *I had better stop before I draw blood,* she thought, discarding the paddle and choosing a whip. She flicked it with a resounding crack. "Get up, you horrible little man. Get on your hands and knees and beg for mercy, and while you're at it lick my feet." He rolled over on to his back and she was surprised to see substantial evidence of his pleasure, straining the taut nylon of his skimpy underwear.

When her shock had subsided a little, she thought, *He won't lick my feet, not when he sees my bunions.* But he did, though he hesitated and took some time to adjust to the sight of her misshapen old extremities, to the knobbly toes, the corns and the thickened toenails that she knew were the source of his reluctance. Slowly, he edged forward, lowered his head, and paused once more. *Go on, I'm the boss*, she thought. *Do it, you pusillanimous creep.* "I'll box your ears you don't." It was the wrong thing to say because of course he wanted her to box his ears. He began to get up, until she gave him a hefty clout about the head.

The sensation of his wet tongue on her skin was pleasurable. *This is worth a bob or two,* she told herself. *I must remember this.*

But she wasn't there for her own pleasure, so she followed with one or two commands Evie had recommended. It wasn't so difficult for he was an obliging little man. It would not be true to say a good time was had by both but it was good enough for a first attempt, even if it left Godfrey bemused.

At the end of an hour, and sweating profusely, Madame Dolores cried. "That's enough. Time's up. You can get dressed now. I will hand you over to my colleague, Sue. You can chat to her while you relax with a cup of tea. I hope this session was satisfactory."

Godfrey looked a little subdued but nodded that it was. "How do I pay you?" he asked.

"Give the fee to Miss Sue. I'm not interested in money. Cash, if you don't mind," and she made for the stairs.

Sue was waiting in the hall and took Godfrey into the kitchen where she watched him lower himself gingerly into the only firm chair.

Evie appeared with the tea and offered one of her parsnip muffins, which he declined. "Oh, do have one, they are absolutely delirious. I put some Smarties in them as everyone likes chocolate, don't they."

But he would not be persuaded. Instead he grimaced and squirmed from side to side in an effort to sooth his aching bottom.

Sue watched him sympathetically. "Has she overdone it, Mr Grateful? Miss… I mean Madame Dolores is inclined to be over-enthusiastic sometimes."

"Oh no, it was just fine. A little basic but we can learn together."

"So you mean to come again?"

"Yes, of course. There is n-nowhere else locally we can go."

Who was this "we"? thought Sue, as she watched him fish his glasses out of his pocket and position them on his nose.

"Do you know a lot of people with similar desires who would like to come?"

"Oh loads. I'll p-pass the word around, if you like."

Thirteen

In her bedroom, Dorothy removed her motley and put on her normal clothes. She knew she had looked a fright but hoped the dim lighting had hidden the worst features of her disguise. She was worried that Godfrey was dissatisfied with her efforts; the session had been a few minutes short of an hour because she had run out of ideas of what to do. She could have tied him up or actually whipped him or made him do something unspeakably humiliating, except that she couldn't think what. Clearly more research was needed if he came again. She must mug up on the flogging and the bondage. What surprised her the most, however, was how enjoyable the whole time had been for her, once her nerves had gone. It was lovely lashing out with that paddle and the foot licking was sensational. It made her ask the question – had she been hiding these proclivities all her life? How sad to find out her true nature so late in the day, after a lifetime of suppressing hidden pleasures out of inhibition and ignorance.

Sue and Evie were waiting in the lounge to find out how the session went. Eagerly, they sat up to question her as soon as she came downstairs.

"How did it go? Did you have to tie him up and spank him?" Evie leaned forward as she spoke, anticipating a fulsome description of what had gone on. Dorothy, however, was fearful that she had not done well, and refused to go into details.

"I am like a doctor with a patient. It is all confidential. All I will say is that he seemed to enjoy himself. I certainly did."

"What was he like?"

Sue could answer that. "He was very normal and quite ordinary. We had a pleasant chat and he promised to tell other men about us. He asked if we were new to the business and I had to admit that we were. He said he would be glad to see us "expand our range", whatever that meant."

"He refused one of my muffins," Evie complained.

"He told me he was allergic to parsnips. You'll have to cook something more palatable, Evie."

Evie laughed. "Goodness yes. The last thing we want to cope with is his antarctic shock. Oh, have I got that right?"

"No, dear, but we know what you mean," Sue replied.

Sue then asked Dorothy what they really wanted to know. "But will you do it again if more callers come?"

Her reply surprised them. "Yes, as long as they don't ask me to do anything really improper."

This was the answer Sue and Evie had been hoping for. If more clients were as normal and ordinary as Godfrey everything could proceed swimmingly. Today there were £32 extra pounds in the desk drawer, and with luck, more to come.

Sue was thoughtful. She was wondering if she could develop her role into something she could charge for. The term "agony aunt" had just dropped into the conversation earlier. In the absence of proper qualifications, it would describe her well enough. To the others, she said, "You know, we have all lived a long life and we have been around the houses, as they say. We have seen it all —well, I have – family problems, relationships going wrong, broken hearts, errant children. I am in an ideal position to give advice, aren't I?"

"Good thinking." Dorothy nodded her agreement, but Evie wanted to know how she also could contribute.

"Chef, waitress and secretary, isn't that enough for you?"

"I suppose. I can write the letters and I'll certainly look up some more palatial recipes.

"Palatable!" the other two chorused.

The days went by and there was no knock on the door from a potential client. They wondered if they should choose another man from the list and write another letter, but just as they decided, their skills were required by a huge giant of a man, just the kind that Dorothy dreaded. After all, he was likely to hit back with his great fists if she threatened him with a cane.

His name was Tony, AKA Twostroke, and a nicer chap did not exist.

"Hello there, ma'am, I'm a friend of Godfrey and he said you could help me."

"I will do my best." This time Dorothy had eschewed the fancy togs and wore a severe blouse and skirt.

In the boot room, she asked him what he wanted.

"I like being a pupil. You look just like my teacher. I need to be kept in order because I am often very naughty."

Ah, thought Dorothy, *role play, that's right up my street,* and she picked out a suitable cane and said, "I don't tolerate naughtiness in my class, so mind your Ps and Qs. Stand in the corner and recite your ABC."

She stood in front of him, legs apart, holding the cane at each end, flexing it as if preparing to strike. He started on his ABC but soon began to blubber.

Dorothy frowned. Was this real? "What's the matter? Why are you crying?"

Tears rolled down through the grooves in his fleshy face."My mummy doesn't love me and my daddy has gone away."

Dorothy was nonplussed. Could she lay into this sad man-child with the cane? Surely not. In her ordinary voice she said, "What do you want me to do now?"

"A cuddle would be nice. I'll feel better after a cuddle."

Dorothy didn't usually cuddle. She hadn't cuddled anyone for years. Was this another thing she would have to learn?

"Oh, come on then. Sit on the chaise longue and I'll give you a cuddle."

So that is what they did. After a while she drew his sorry head to her breast and they just sat. He got a bit exploratory after a while, but she didn't mind. *When people are as old as I am,* she told herself, *no one touches us at all, and in the privacy of the red room, I must learn to put up with anything.*

Luckily, his probing never went too far, and at the end of the session, explorer and exploree went away feeling buoyant.

Sue enjoyed the gentle giant too. He told her his wife had left him so she sympathised and listened to his woes until he felt better. Evie did not appear with tea so they both went to the kitchen and made it together. He went on his way comforted.

Where had Evie gone? It puzzled both Sue and Dorothy when they sat together after the client's departure. She had never said she was going out. "Perhaps she got tired of making palatial muffins," laughed Sue.

"Dereliction of duty," declared Dorothy. "I shall have to have words."

"I think she feels a little left out, now that you are the domme and her expertise is not needed."

Dorothy said nothing; she did not consider herself a professional but reckoned that with the increase in clients, she could work things out for herself.

Evie was evasive when she turned up. "Oh, just here and there," she replied when asked where she had been. "You can manage without me for a bit, can't you?" I left some carrot and gorgonzola cheese stores in the oven. Didn't you find them?"

Fourteen

Godfrey soon proved his usefulness and it wasn't long before they were booking two clients a day and the money was rolling in. Two a day was Dorothy's limit, for the "work" took it out of her, she said. Godfrey was a regular and very soon became more of a friend, as did some of their other regulars. Evie came and went, a law unto herself and they stopped asking her where she went on those afternoons.

Often Dorothy mused about this new activity she had taken up. "It is very strange. If I scold or threaten punishments, their eyes light up. That is exactly what they want. I have to refuse to flog them or chain them up to make them beg for it. "Hurt me, please," they say. Very odd."

The next time Godfrey came, he brought a smart riding crop. "What's that for?" Dorothy asked. "I've got canes galore here."

"It's b-better for six of the b-best, and this time I want you to t-tie me up until it hurts."

If that was what he wanted she was happy to oblige. Another client, aka Sixpack, proved less gung-ho than his name suggested, and wanted to be slapped, restrained all over with parcel tape and shoved in a dark cupboard until he begged to be released. Madame Dolores was happy to do that too and then went to the lounge to join Sue in a cup of tea.

Sue put down her book, *Counselling For Dummies,* and told Dorothy she admired the way she was coping with her new career.

"I know, I've been experimenting with different ways of tying them up. The collars are proving popular, especially if I drag them around the room on a lead."

"What did you want all those aerosol cans of cream for?"

"Ah, that would be my "creamy treats." I taunt them with a cream bun, make them beg for it."

"And do you give it to them?"

"Not exactly. I smear it over me and make him lick it off. Then I give it to them."

"Goodness. So where do you smear it exactly?"

"Don't ask, Sue. Just don't ask."

"What is all that thumping and knocking we can hear on occasions?"

"That will be Peter Poker. He likes me to hurl things at him. I started with ping pong balls but they didn't hurt enough so I moved on to golf balls."

"You are being creative, I must say, but don't go too far, Dorothy. We don't want to be too cruel."

"Don't worry. They tell me I'm one of the best."

Sue gave a satisfied smile. "Well, it is certainly bringing in the cash but do be careful. We don't want any accidents."

"Oh, I know when to stop, believe me."

"Where is Mr Sixpack? You've been here for almost fifteen minutes."

"I left him trussed up in the cupboard. He wanted some sensory deprivation. He will yell when he's had enough."

"How can he yell if you've taped his mouth?"

Dorothy jumped up. "Golly, you are right. I'd better go and release him before he expires."

After several successful months, Dorothy asked herself why there were so many men so eager to be tortured. She learned from Sue that most were failures in some way or had a variety of problems. It was as if they needed to be punished for their failure even when, in the outside world, they were deemed to be successful. In the lives they had chosen, or had forced upon them, they strived to earn, to achieve, to be accepted. She concluded that the pressure of all that striving and the pretence made them unconsciously unhappy. Their time with her was an escape from their untrue lives into something more simple and true. The pain and the hu-

miliation was an acknowledgment of what they believed they deserved.

Of course, there were some who came, enjoyed the
pain and the resulting arousal and left satisfied, but
Dorothy realised she occupied a niche in this odd
world. Lame ducks were becoming her speciality but
she had a sneaking suspicion that Sue was mostly
responsible for that. They came to talk to Sue and the
domme time with her was merely the *hors d'oeuvre*.

Not inclined to think about her own failure, her
need to control and dominate, Dorothy was only glad
they could now afford to sort out the house. One of the
showers had been installed and they used it in turn. The
roof had been fixed and several useful electrical
devices were bought and fitted.

With no man permanently in the house and Odd Job
Bob being so unreliable, their client friends were
always ready to step in and help. When a load of heavy
compost bags was delivered to their front door, Mr
Twostroke carried them through to the garden. When
the back door got stuck and no one could get into the
garden, Mr Buffalo Bill sorted it out. If by chance a
booking over-ran and there were two clients in the
house at the same time, they all had tea together and
anonymity went out of the window. It became clear

that a number of the men knew each other well. Life was becoming very social and the women loved it.

It was too good to last. Evie was off somewhere and Dorothy took it into her head to hang a poster on the lounge wall. It was a print of a chorus line of Folies Bergère dancers doing high kicks.

"Why that one?" asked Sue.

"It's a classic by that little painter, Toulouse Lautrec. It will give the impression that we are not just aging tarts but have a modicum of culture."

Sue looked a bit doubtful, especially when Dorothy dragged up a chair and climbed on it. "I thought you had given up climbing. Do be careful."

"Stop fussing, Sue, and fetch me a hammer. This blue-tack is useless."

Sue was hunting in the kitchen drawers, when she heard an almighty crash and a cry of pain. Rushing back, she found Dorothy on the floor and the chair overturned.

"I told you," she cried, while helping a red-faced Dorothy to sit.

Gasping with the effort, Dorothy put her hand on to the floor to lever herself up, but as she leaned she gave a scream and pulled her arm in close to her chest. "I think it's broken. God, that hurts."

"Maybe you've just sprained it."

"I know the difference between a sprain and a break, you stupid woman. It's my right hand too. How will I be able to do the necessary in the red room now?"

"Do stop wailing, Dorothy. We'll bind it up and I'll take you to the surgery."

Sue rang for a taxi. The surgery advised an X-Ray so they went to the hospital and waited several hours for that to be done. It was indeed a break, a complex one, and Dorothy would be *hors de combat* for at least six weeks.

They had to cancel all the bookings and for several weeks they had no income. Then one or two of their most friendly customers drifted back on the pretext of talking to Sue. Those who had problems still needed her wise words or just her listening presence. It brought in a few pounds but Dorothy's earnings were sorely missed.

Evie was sympathetic but also warned that if Dorothy was unavailable for too long, the men might find an alternative service. Somehow, they must find a way of fortifying their communications network lest they were forgotten.

"You are getting technical in your old age," Dorothy said. "*Fortifying our communications network* indeed. Who have you been talking to?"

"I have my contacts." Evie stuck her nose in the air and would say no more.

The problem gave them cause for a lot of thought. "We could send round a letter to all our regulars and tell them what's happened. They can come back in six weeks."

"That's time enough to forget anything," grumbled Dorothy. "I can't remember what I did yesterday, and how can I be sure the break will be really strong enough in six weeks?"

Evie said, "Why don't we have a party? Get everyone together in a week or two. A Vicars and Tarts party!"

"A party? How can we three have a party with ten men, you silly woman?"

"The men could bring their wives and just tell them we were old friends. We could ask other friends and relations too. That would mix them all up a bit." explained Evie.

Sue said, "But why would we be doing this? None of us has a birthday yet."

Evie laughed. "Daddy and I never needed a reason to have a party. It would cement our ties with the clients, don't you think?"

Dorothy groaned. "Does it have to be a Vicars and Tarts?"

"But why not? It's very appropriate."

In the absence of any other idea, they agreed to have a party, but not a Vicars and Tarts. Sue and Evie were keen, but Dorothy vetoed it. If they did ask relations and friends, most would surely be disgusted at the idea and refuse to come. And what could their old age pensioner friends wear as a tart when all they had in the wardrobe these days were woollies and bed socks?

"We should just call it an At Home. It will look good on an invitation: *Dorothy, Sue and Evie invite you to their At Home. Dress: casual and bring a bottle.*"

"Can't we afford any booze?"

"No, we cannot. We can provide soft drinks. The food will cost us enough."

"Leave that to me," cried Evie. "I have some lovely finger food recipes."

"As long as there is no actual fingers in what you make," Sue said, nudging Dorothy when she muttered that she wouldn't be surprised.

Finally, they decided that nuts and crisps would do."

Dorothy added, "I'm going to buy some candles – we must save on electricity, otherwise the lights will be on till the early hours."

Sue frowned. "Do you think we should? Accidents do happen and there will be a lot of people in this room."

Evie clapped her hands. "Oh yes, candles are so romantic. We must have some."

Dorothy looked at the woman who had never paid an electricity bill in her life. "They will all be sensible adults, old enough to be careful."

"I hope you are right. I had a friend once who left a little mirror on her window sill. The sun incited the curtains and the fire burned all through her bedroom."

Sue smiled and gave Evie a tolerant pat on the shoulder. "Did they, dear."

"Well, we must remember not to leave any sort of mirror around, ok? And I think we should put a donation box by the front door." This was Dorothy's final contribution to the discussion, but Sue and Evie put their feet firmly down on that.

"We are not collecting for a charity so it would look like begging," Sue said. "The idea is to keep our contacts alive."

Dorothy grumbled under her breath about an opportunity lost, but having won over the candles, she had to give way.

The evening of the party arrived and the three waited with great anticipation to see who would come. By way of preparation, one or two of the more serviceable garments had graduated from the once locked room to put them in a party mood, so under their workaday clothes, Sue and Dorothy wore more exotic but never-to-be-seen items. A red plastic bra crackled mysteriously under Sue's blouse, while Dorothy persevered with what she called her "miniknicks", even though every time she sat down she felt she was in danger of being sliced in two.

Evie had laid out the buffet and disappeared. It was a relief to them both as they were afraid she would turn up dressed in a mix of garments from the upstairs room and embarrass half the guests while provoking the rest to scandalous behaviour.

Mr Grateful arrived first and then Sixpack, and Thunderbum with Bigboy in tow.

Sue was on tenterhooks, having invited her son and Frightful Flora to the party. They arrived and as Sue led them into the lounge, she heard Jerry's murmur of surprise to see so many strange men in the gathering.

"Who are all these weirdos?" Flora whispered.

"Search me," Jerry replied.

Flora went to peruse the buffet, doubting there was anything edible because she had recently become a vegan.

Evie had excelled herself. There were plum and parsley rolls, little ginger biscuits iced with salad cream, sardines marinated in golden syrup, a cake studded with prunes and peppers and her famous almond and gorgonzola cheese straws.

"Mm, interesting," Flora decided, because it all looked good, but when she had done with tasting and was full of vodka, it took three visits to the downstairs loo before she felt right again.

Soon the party was in full swing. Mavis had come with a cohort of her dancing pupils and they all had a noisy reunion. Mavis, as their spokesperson, declared the three were sorely missed at the Community Centre. She was one pound fifty pence short every Wednesday since The Holy Trinity's absence but she didn't like to mention that. "If I'd thought, I would have brought some music and we could have done a dance or two, just to jog your memories, you know. Is there anyone coming this evening who might like to join our happy little band?"

Sue looked around the room. Fancy Flora? Mrs Odd Job Bob? Bunged Up Bertie's wife? No, too feeble, too fat and too frumpy. She shook her head.

"Oh well, never mind. Come on girls, let's get pissed."

Odd Job Bob's wife came dressed in the only finery she had: a dress in a colourful jungle pattern that enhanced her substantial cleavage and drew the eyes of all the men like homing pigeons. Bunged Up Bertie's wife looked vague, frazzle-haired and hugely pregnant so she sat throughout the evening.

The request to bring a bottle had been duly observed and soon every ledge, shelf and windowsill held bottles of gin, vodka and whiskey and a variety of liqueurs. Dorothy had put on what she supposed was suitable party music; a compilation of folk songs from Albania, but it was soon changed and Abba's *Dancing Queen* had everyone on their feet.

By the time Sue and Dorothy were incapable of any sensible reaction, the whole house was over-run by the guests searching for the bathrooms. These were generously put to use, sometimes urgently so. Godfrey decided to take forty winks on Evie's bed and one or two others found their way into what was still called "the locked room". Sue had remembered to lock the boot room door but had not supposed anyone would venture upstairs. Within a short time, Mr Thunderbum and a friend burst into the lounge, dressed in a grotesque variety of leather and vinyl garments. They struck a flamboyant pose that had half the room delirious with laughter. The other half, such as Mavis's dancers, and one or two other outsiders, stood riveted to the spot, eyes popping, drinks held frozen before gaping mouths.

"Oh, I say, that's going a bit far, don't you think? Should we all have come in fancy dress?" someone was heard to say.

"Don't look, girls," advised Mavis to the more fragile of her dancers. "The sight will keep you awake for weeks."

"Oo, so that's what a drag queen looks like. I've never seen a real one."

"Stop staring, Esme, you'll embarrass them."

There were eight men in the room pretending a casual lack of interest. "Some people will do anything to get attention. Pure attention-seeking, that's what it is," BigBoy said. "Come on everyone, how about a rousing chorus of *What's New Pussycat?*"

By this time Sue was sitting on Mr Sixpack's lap and Dorothy was curled up on the sofa, snoring contentedly.

Evie was less inebriated than most because her friend Giles had arrived and she was keen to introduce him to Sue and Dorothy. Giles was at least as old as she was but feisty with it. He sported a huge moustache but with rather less hair on his head. Together they were having a good time as the walking stick he used was pushed and poked into all sorts of places, making them both laugh uproariously. As the strains of the singsong gave way to a heightened level of chatter, the couple stumbled upon Dorothy, who was clearly not in listening mode, so they wandered among the guests until they found Sue.

"There you are. We've been looking everywhere for you. This is my friend Giles and we have something to tell you."

Sue hiccupped. "Well, here I am." She was bleary-eyed, and indicated she was listening but without any guarantee of either understanding or remembering what Evie chose to tell her.

"I'm leaving the house. This is Giles and I'm decamping into the Care Home with him. I want you to pass the message along to Dorothy."

A mild glimmer of alarm shot over Sue's face. "Which house?"

"This house, of course."

"Why?"

"Because they appreciate me there. My song and dance act goes down a storm and they have offered me a room."

Sue was frowning and screwing up her face in an effort to take in this news. "When?"

"Oh, very soon, when the paperwork is complete."

"Okay, I'll tell Dorothy. Bye," and she waved a limp hand in Evie's direction and lowered her head to continue tracing the tattoos on Mr Sixpack's chest with a gentle finger, while he panted a little and squirmed beneath her.

"I think she's discovered one of his anonymous zones," Evie whispered to Giles.

As midnight approached, the guests began to drift off home. The candles had done their job and there were now dollops of wax where they had burned down. Only one remained alight, flickering into the darkness of the party room, empty except for a snoozing Dorothy. It was on the mantelpiece above the smouldering embers of the fire. The room had become over-warm during the dancing and someone had opened a window.

Now, a cool evening breeze made the flame flare and caught an RSVP card standing nearby. At first there was only a scorch mark but the second time it happened the card burst into flame, tipped over and fell to the hearth below, landing on a crumpled paper serviette. When the flames from this caught the corner of a discarded cushion that then set the easy chair alight, the room began to smell of burning. A thin white smoke spread about the room.

Dorothy slept on. When the fire alarm finally sounded, she shot up in a fright. Befuddled and hungover, she pushed aside her blanket and tried to stand. It wasn't easy because she was dizzy and could see little through the thickening pall of smoke, but alarmed, she staggered out of the room to the bottom of the stairs.

She shouted for Sue, but it came out as a croak. Again she shouted, and began to mount the stairs, the urgency of the situation becoming clearer by the minute. Grey smoke was pouring out of the door of the lounge and she felt a blast of heat on her back. "Sue, wake up. We are all going to die!"

Sue came out on to the landing in her striped PJs. "What the…?" That was as far as she got. She rushed down the staircase to where Dorothy stood and grabbed her arm. "We've got to get out of here. Come on." She hauled Dorothy into the kitchen and closed the door. "We'll be safer outside."

They stood on the patio and turned to look back. In the depths of the house, flames were visible.

"Where's Evie?" Dorothy's eyes were wide with horror. "Is she still in bed?"

Sudden realisation hit Sue. She put her hand over her mouth. "We must get her out!"

They both turned and rushed back into the kitchen where, having shut the door, very little smoke had penetrated. Dorothy grabbed the handle and wrenched the door open, only to be met by a huge cloud of smoke that engulfed her, making her eyes water and a rasping cough emerge from her anguished lungs. There was no way she could see the stairs. A roaring noise told her the fire had spread. No one could get up those stairs to save Evie.

She slammed the door shut. "Ring 999, Sue, quickly!"

Sue sobbed. "I can't. You do it. I haven't got my phone on me."

"On the landline, you fool. I can't, my hand is useless. Hurry up or it will be too late!"

Fifteen

Anonymous firemen in their fireproof uniforms doused the flames with their water hoses and much of the rest of the house too. Meanwhile the two women sat in the garden, utterly distraught. They had rushed unthinking from the conflagration with no thought for anyone but themselves. Fear had provoked panic and now the consequences obsessed their minds.

"What have we done?" Sue's expression was of horror, her mouth distorted, her eyes wide.

"What have we not done?" Dorothy grimly replied. She was shaking, undermined by the knowledge of her unforgivable selfishness

"Why didn't I go and wake her? It was the vodka," wailed Sue, doubled up on the bench with self-reproach and guilt.

"She was always a sound sleeper. Do you think she was aware she was being burnt to death?"

"Oh, oh, don't say that. It's all our fault. We didn't think, just panicked and thought of our own safety."

Dorothy bent over as if racked with pain. "I feel awful, just awful. I was so mean to her." Dorothy's face was white and her hands were clasped around her stomach

"She didn't mind – you are mean to everyone. I saw her, you know, with a big fellow called Giles. She gave me a message for you."

"For me? Oh, that makes me feel worse. What message?"

Sue told her all she could remember of the exchange during the party.

Dorothy sat back. "Leaving us? Oh God, she has hasn't she, she's truly left us. She surely didn't mean… How could she know?"

"No, no, I don't mean the fire. She was going to join that Giles chap in his Care Home."

But Dorothy shook her head. "No. She wouldn't, not after all we've been through together."

"Well, she was."

"Sorry and goodbye, was it?" Dorothy said bitterly. "It will be our job to tell this Giles she's gone."

Sue let her tears fall unheeded. "Everyone will be upset. I'm upset. Evie was liked by everyone except you. She was always happy and full of fun. I can't bear to think of it. Everyone will call us murderers."

Dorothy rocked back and forth, frowning. "I wasn't nasty to her all the time."

"Go on, admit it: it was most of the time."

"She was our friend, one of us. Oh, why was I so cruel to her? I'll never forgive myself. Never."

Dorothy continue to rock back and forth, moaning to herself. When the firemen had drenched everything in sight and had begun to pack up their hoses, they were still sitting in a state of nervous exhaustion in the garden. The head fireman approached and they shrank from his look as he removed his goggles and helmet.

"You are fortunate, ladies, that we came in time and stopped the fire reaching the upper floor."

They looked at each other and then at him. "But the woman upstairs, how did she die? Was it the smoke?" Sue hardly dare look at the accusation she knew was in his face.

"Smoke inhalation is certainly a killer if anybody had been up there. But we found no body."

The two women wailed in concert. "Burnt to a crisp. Oh we can't bear to think of it."

The fireman shook his head. "Nope, nobody burnt."

Dorothy suddenly stood up. "But where is she then if she was not burned?"

"Who? I told you, there was no body up there. The rooms were empty, they smell bad but otherwise were untouched."

Both women were speechless. If Evie had not been burned to a crisp, and hadn't even been there,   where was she? "Have you looked in ALL the rooms?" said

Sue. It would be just like Evie to go and hide from the flames!

"Of course. We made a 100% search of the premises. We can't leave even a matchstick smouldering. That would be a potential fire hazard. Sorry about the mess." And with that he turned to join his team waiting by their engine to hurry back to the station.

Dorothy sat up, every muscle taut. "What? Not dead? How like that thoughtless woman. Just wait till I see her. She has really put us through the hell."

"But Dorothy, she couldn't have known about the fire. We can't blame her. To be honest I am relieved, aren't you? She must have gone off with Nigel or Giles or whatever his name is."

"I suppose so. Yes, of course I'm glad. Now I can tell her what I think of her."

"You've changed your mind a bit quick," Sue said. "What about all the regret you felt a minute ago"

"That was when I thought she was dead. Now I realise she has betrayed us, killed our dream. We were a team, working for the good of each other and she goes off by herself and makes other arrangements, secretly, selfishly looking after herself. Not a word to us. She even lied to us."

"Did she? How did she lie?"

Mocking Evie's sweet little voice, Dorothy said, *"Oh, I've been here and there.* That was a lie."

"Perhaps it was true at the time."

"That woman has as much relation with the truth as a... pig in a poke."

"Pig in a poke means..."

"Oh, shut up, Susan."

Sue could not understand this rapid change of mood. She stared at Dorothy's angry expression and wondered if the woman would ever regret, or even remember, her sorrow when she thought Evie was dead. She said, "So now you don't regret being horrible to her and driving her out?"

"Me? Driving her out? Why do you say such an awful thing." She clamped her mouth shut and sat for long thoughtful minutes while Sue watched her, hoping that with luck she was pondering the truth in that remark.

When they both felt up to it, they stumbled around what was left of the ground floor of the house. The kitchen was intact, the boot room and the hall reeked of smoke and the walls were streaked with grey stains. The lounge was a sodden mess with scorched walls, the rugs, chairs and sofa hideously deformed and coloured in a depressing shade of black. The Folies Bergère still

166

hung askew on the wall with its former gaiety somewhat dimmed. Some of the curtains had survived but the rest hung in tatters. How could they live with all the wreckage, the damp and the mess? It would take months for the smoke smell to disappear.

"What are we going to do?" Sue moaned. "Do you think it is repairable?"

"Not by us, I can tell you that. We haven't that sort of money. And I'm not going to live in the kitchen and sleep in those bedrooms. I've got more respect for my lungs."

"So are we going to end up in the Care Home after all?"

"Never," growled Dorothy. "I'll go on the streets first."

Sue was considering her options but could think of only one. She would have to go back to her old home and live with Jerry and Flora. They surely would not refuse to take her in. She would hate it, but what else was there? She decided to pay a visit and throw herself on their mercy.

She knew Dorothy had no options and she felt a mite sorry. Would her friend really have to go on the streets? Her cottage was gone along with her furniture and so were all her savings. Her new skill would be useless. How would it sound at the employment agency if she enquired about vacancies for a dominatrix?

Not wanting to talk to Flora, Sue waited until the evening when Jerry would be home from work. She wasn't sure what he did in Fogerty's these days although he did say his promotion had come through. When he answered her call, she cried, "Jerry, there has been a terrible disaster and I need your help,"

"What kind of disaster?" He sounded cagey.

"I would rather not say over the phone, but I need to come over and talk to you about it."

They were free the next day, which was none too soon for Sue, as time spent in the house was intolerable and worry about her future filled every waking moment.

On Saturday morning, she approached her old home. It looked different somehow. How could she forget so soon the details of a house where she had spent so many years? The pink paint had gone; that was it, and there were blinds at the windows instead of the lovely yellow and rust curtains that she had run up herself.

Jerry answered the door. "Now then, what's this disaster you mentioned?"

"Let me get in first," she said, pushing past him into the hall, her feet sinking into unexpected softness. "Oh, you've carpeted the hall!" She followed him into the kitchen that now was entirely different, for a wall between the dining room and the kitchen had gone.

"We prefer open plan living," he said when he saw her surprised face.

"Oh, you never said."

"Flora's idea. She has strong views on interior decor."

She has strong views on everything, thought Sue. "It looks very smart. I like the large table and the plain grey cabinets."

Flora came in from the lounge. "Hello Susan, you look a bit frantic."

"Do I? That's because I have some terrible news."

"Oh dear," she said, moving to the sink. "Jerry, take this tub down to the compost bin, will you? And the water bucket here needs emptying. Pour it on the peas."

Jerry paused but clearly did not dare delay. He disappeared into the garden.

"We are collecting waste water for the plants and the composting cuts down on the food waste," Flora explained. "Not that there's much of that, now that we have become an eco house."

"What is an eco house?"

"It means we recycle, reuse and repair."

"That's very commendable, I suppose."

"But of course it is. Don't you do the same?" She spoke as if this was obvious to any idiot.

"Not any more," Sue said, and Flora tutted loudly.

When he returned from the garden, Jerry picked up the kettle and began to fill it from the tap. Flora leapt up at once. "Three cupfuls only, Jerry. That's all we need." She turned to Sue. "We use less electricity now. We turn off the heating most of the time."

"Won't you be cold in the winter?" Sue knew all about this.

"What is wrong with thick woollen jumpers? I have knitted them for both of us."

They took three cups of coffee into the lounge. A plate with three biscuits came too. Sue found the odd flavour was not to her liking.

"Don't worry, they won't make you fat." Flora must have noticed Sue's frown. "I made them this morning. They are fat-free and sugar-free with herbs and chicory."

Come back Evie, all is forgiven, passed through Sue's mind.

Jerry said, "Now, Mum, tell us what has happened."

Sue sat on the edge of a chair. "The house is burnt, not quite to the ground, but we had a fire and it is unliveable-in."

They both stared at her. "But we were there only a couple of days ago. It was alright then."

"It was after the party," and she told them both the events of that night, finally saying, "So you see, we have all got to move out. It's in a terrible state and we can't afford to repair it. I have to find somewhere else to live and my first thought was you. Could you take me in? For a short while?"

Flora had fixed a stony gaze on Sue and then said, "You mean move in with us!?" And she exchanged a glance with Jerry.

"Er, Mum, we've changed things around. Your rooms are now my office and Flora's craft room. And we divided your bedroom into a dressing room for us both."

Sue listened to this and her heart sank. No room for a nursery, never mind a lodger. And if she wasn't mistaken, there was a dog's basket and bowl right by the kitchen door. Strange, because Jerry hated dogs.

"What about the third bedroom, the guest room that was?"

Flora coughed and looked again at Jerry. "Yes, that's still there," he said.

"Then couldn't you put me up just for a little while until I find somewhere else? I've got no money, you see, it all went into buying the house." Her voice tailed off. No doubt Flora would describe the tension in the room as a negative vibe.

"If you have no resources, your "little while" might be longer than you think. Have you really no other option? What are your two friends going to do?"

"Evie has linked up with a man she's fond of. And Dorothy is still considering her options."

Warning glances were being exchanged. Sue was dismayed. "I wouldn't take up much room and I could be very useful about the house, cleaning and cooking, that sort of thing."

Jerry's face lit up. "Ah, your apple dumplings. How I've missed your apple dumplings."

Flora shuddered. "Dumplings, what a terrible choice! Jerry you are forgetting our ethos. Dumplings, indeed."

Eager to get out of the house as soon as possible, Sue said, "So will you think about it?" Reluctance oozed all around her and she had no hope of any outcome that she would enjoy, but she was desperate.

Jerry was looking concerned. "Stay for lunch, Mum, and we can thrash this out some more."

Out of polite interest, Sue asked what they were having. "Roast carrots and turnips" was the reply.

"Thank you but no." She had to go, to avoid bursting into tears in front of them both.

Sixteen

Back in the garden of Eyesore Towers, Sue told Dorothy there was no hope of a billet with Jerry and Flora.

"What a miserable ungrateful pair," Dorothy cried.

Sue sighed. "Well, in a way I can understand it. Who really wants an old biddy living with them. It's an open commitment. It might be different if they had a granny flat to offer."

"No, but really, you gave them your house, a whole house, and I bet they have increased it's value quite a bit already."

"I can't say I am too disappointed. I'm not sure I could stand watching Flora order Jerry about. You should see her; a patchwork shift she obviously made herself, nuts and seeds necklace and straw sandals. The house is littered with driftwood, shells and stones. I bet they save brown paper and bits of string, no plastic in sight and no meat to eat, ugh. But I'd like to know what they have done with all my Capo Di Monte."

"At least you have someone to ask. Who have I got?"

"But Dorothy, you have two daughters, sorry, stepdaughters. Why not try them?"

"They both live in someone else's house. They can't make the decision to take me in."

"Then go to whoever does own it. Is it a big place?"

"The Hall? Yes, but we have history. I'm not sure that a request from me would get a favourable response."

"Why, what happened?"

"It's a long story. I thought I was doing the right thing but it wasn't."

"It was the wrong thing? Tell me about it."

"Haven't you had enough of counselling the walking wounded?"

"Is that how you think of yourself?"

Dorothy pulled a face. "I'm coming round to that view."

"Nevertheless, your girls would give you a hearing, wouldn't they?"

"They might, but if they can't do anything, what's the point?"

"Dorothy, you have so little faith in people. How could it hurt to try? You might be surprised."

Dorothy added depression to her morose mood, but she knew what Sue would say if she rejected her suggestion. She didn't mind talking to the younger Kitty who was alright, but Clare was a bit of a dragon. Where had she learned to be so hard? Her heart sank and she slumped in her chair, for she knew the answer. It was her own example that had taught Clare, during all the years of their growing up. She had actually enjoyed the animosity between them when she had the power and the authority. There was no fun to be had from Kitty, who crumpled and cried at every cross word. Not so Clare, who had encouraged Kitty marry and then to leave her husband. Kitty had always followed her sister's lead, especially when her husband turned out to be a misunderstood, damaged young man. Simon was the son of Clare's boss, the owner of the Hall, and she herself had championed the boy and never believed he was the monster they said he was. She had even visited him in prison for a few years. He told her the truth, well, his truth, and for the sympathy and support she had given him, Clare had never forgiven her.

Now, knowing what he did to Kitty, Clare was unlikely to be sympathetic or do much to help, although it had to be said that it was she who had persuaded her boss to pay for the boiler, now lying idle in the cupboard opposite the famous locked room.

"Okay, I'll go," she told Sue. "I'll phone tomorrow."

"Do it now. Anyone would think you were afraid of her."

It was true, she was, but she wasn't going to appear a coward in front of Sue or anyone.

Kitty answered the phone. "Dorothy, this is a surprise. How are you?"
Instead of replying to that, and to steady her nerve, Dorothy enquired about everyone at the Hall,
the staff, Gordon the boss, and Frankie the child.

"Gordon is well, Maggie and Stan are well too. Everyone is well. We have two new staff and Frankie is growing up fast."

"So you have a houseful."

"Eight of us now, quite a little community. Have you been to visit Simon recently? I heard he is due for parole soon."

"I haven't been for years."

When they had exhausted all the pleasantries, Dorothy told Kitty the bare bones of her situation.

"Our own experiment in communal living was not as successful as yours obviously is. We now have to separate and find our own places to live. I'm looking around to see what's available and I wondered if you or Clare had any suggestions." Her voice came out more plaintively than she wanted. "I'm not as active as I was and I have no transport. I thought I should come and talk it over with you and Clare."

"Would you like me to acquaint Clare of what you say? It would give her time to think. She isn't here at the moment but I believe tomorrow afternoon would be a good time."

Dorothy said that would be fine, and put the phone down, surprised to find that her hands were shaking. If talking to Kitty had this effect, what would talking to Clare be like? Her ward was not a girl any more; she was in her late forties now, virtually running the estate since her boss Gordon's heart attack. That was some years ago but Clare still did everything to make his life easy.

She turned briskly to join Sue in the garden and suddenly felt her head spin and had to grab a chair-back to steady herself. A fall would be the last straw. It was the stress. It was getting to her.

A taxi dropped Dorothy at the door of the Hall the next afternoon. It looked pretty much the same as she re-membered. There was more greenery; the trees and bushes had doubled in size and a climber now covered a large section of the front of the building. There was a small boy's bicycle in the hall and a pile of shoes and Wellington boots by the door. The kitchen, when she looked in, was more cluttered and there was a strong smell of fish, presumably from their lunch.

Clare came from the lounge to greet her. Her hair was shorter and she was showing her age. Maturity had given her a few wrinkles but those Dorothy saw were no match for her own abundant crop.

"Hello," Clare said, unsmiling. "Come into the lounge and Ruth will bring us some tea."

They sat opposite each other. Dorothy was disarmed by the lack of warmth in Clare's greeting. Perhaps it had not been a good idea to alert her to the purpose of the visit.

A scatter of leaflets on the coffee table caught Clare's attention and she began tidying them. "Well then, tell me what has happened to your house."

Sounding rather stilted, Dorothy explained about the fire, the damage, and how the three of them were now virtually homeless. She paused in the telling for Clare had her attention on the leaflets and Dorothy wondered if she was listening.

"Is it really as bad as that?"

"You could come and see for yourself. You would be shocked."

"I might just do that," Clare said. "Kitty said you thought we might have some suggestions but I honestly can't think of anything. What I do know is that there is no room here, not now that we have extra people.

You'll just have to do the best you can with what's left of your property."

Smart as a whip, Dorothy said, "Live in the shed, you mean."

"No, of course not, but there must be some corner, some part of the structure still standing."

"If you saw the place, you would see what a ridiculous idea that was."

"Oh, come on, Dorothy, you always did exaggerate. I bet it's not that bad."

"Well, you wouldn't know, would you?" Dorothy snapped.

There were several moments of silence while they stared at one another.

It was true the house was not actually flattened. Apart from the smell, which was lessening as the wind blew through the shattered windows, the kitchen and the bedrooms were reasonable. It was just that Dorothy had never expected to consider living in two rooms among all the wreckage and debris. There was minimal and intermittent electricity, a dicey water supply, no heating, and enough holes in the fabric to allow access to all the wildlife that felt inclined to take up residence. No person looking at the house would consider it habitable or even safe.

"So you can't help me."

"Sorry. We are remote here and the information you want does not come our way. And anyway, it was a crazy idea buying a clapped-out ruin at your age. I'm afraid you'll just have to do what you can."

Dorothy felt a flush suffuse her face. Why was she here, begging for help from this hard-hearted woman who, it might be said, at least owed her something? She stood up. "Then there is no point in continuing with this discussion. I shan't waste any more of your time." She might have said more but deep inside, she was aware of the antagonism both Kitty and Clare had endured at her hands. In the general scheme of things, Clare really owed her nothing, especially as Dorothy wasn't a blood relation, despite the title "Aunt" she had forced upon them from their first days together.

As she went out to the waiting taxi, Dorothy felt an unusual swirl of emotions. Not anger, but embarrassment, a feeling of being diminished by the meeting, and desperation because she did not know what she was going to do. Would she be forced at last to enter the Care Home world that she had been so adamantly against? How did one get a place anyway, if one had no money? She would have to stay in the house. Sue would go, and she would be left alone to live like a hermit in a derelict building.

She rubbed her eyes as she went down the steps to the gravel drive. She was not going to cry for the first time in her adult life. She had never cried when her parents died or when Arthur walked out on her. She had worn her anger like a shield, and that is what she would do now.

"How was it?" Sue asked, when they met in the garden.

By this time Dorothy had regained her composure. "The polite brush-off, as I expected."

"I had some news while you were out. It seems my interview with Jerry and Flora has put the wind up them. They are terrified they might have to take me in. I don't know if it is Flora's doing but they are prepared to pay my fees to Sunnyside, if there is a room."

"You will accept that?"

"I must. I can't stay here long term." Sue looked over to the half-demolished sunroom. "Evie phoned and we had a chat. She says Sunnyside is a nice place. She's invited us to their Open Day next weekend. We should go, don't you think?"

"I suppose so," murmured an exhausted Dorothy.

She might as well go. Sunnyside was the only place in the area except for the hospice and at the rate things were going, it wouldn't be long before she was there.

And what did people call care homes? God's waiting room? Could one think of anything more off-putting? However, if Evie and now Sue were prepared to go, she had better find out what all the fuss was about.

There were high iron gates and a long drive to negotiate before reaching Sunnyside. "I expect they are usually closed to stop people escaping," she murmured as they passed through. The building itself was large and imposing, with a lawn in front and a round pond and a fountain where you could drown yourself when you'd had enough. Today there was bunting and pavilions and tables with umbrellas on the lawn and Dorothy had no quarrel with these. It was sunny and hot and she had forgotten her sunhat. If she felt dizzy, as she often did these days, she could always claim it was sunstroke.

Evie, with Giles in tow, was waiting for them.

"Lovely to see you both. Do I need to introduce Giles or did you meet at the party? So glad I avoided the fire. Sue says the house looks terrible. Giles had his wrist slapped for sneaking me in late at night. It was our first night together, wasn't it, you gorgeous hunk?"

Giles harrumphed and looked slightly sheepish and Dorothy's gorge rose at the thought.

Sue said, "So Evie, what's the programme for today?"

"You can enjoy the grounds, see the display of handicrafts and I think there is an Art tent somewhere. Matron will give us all a pep talk at three o"clock and then I'll do my Song and Dance Show while Giles here plays the piano. There will be refreshments in the pavilion. We are expecting quite a crowd."

Evie sounded for all the world as if she was already a long-term resident. *All those afternoons when she had disappeared and wouldn't say where, she must have been here*, thought Dorothy. She had been cementing her relationship with this Giles chap and boring the residents with her "show". They probably slept all through it, then were fulsome in their praise of Evie's efforts when they hadn't actually seen her in action.

As they wandered around the grounds, it was a surprise to see how competent the craft items were. There were lots of knitted hats, doubling as tea cosies, and beautiful knitted toys; bears, penguins, clowns, anything you could think of. Some nimble fingers had produced earrings and pendants. As neither Sue nor Dorothy had been able to thread a needle for years, the tapestries, tray-cloths and placemats were a delight. Not so the paintings in the Art tent.

"What on earth is that?" Sue giggled. "A horse? It looks more like a giant dog. And this one? I wonder who it's supposed to be."

Dorothy was peering at the signature. "It says *Self Portrait*. Gosh, I pity the woman who looks like that."

There were painted stones and large pebbles, some hefty enough to be a weapon should temper get the better of you. There were boxes stuck all over with coloured pictures cut from a magazine.

"Surely these are craft and in the wrong tent," Sue observed.

When they had walked enough and both had become hot and bothered because Dorothy had also forgotten her walking stick and Sue's arthritic hip was playing up, they had tea and cakes in the pavilion. They admired the cakes and each had a slice, hoping it would not turn out to be one of Evie's triumphs. Soon they were joined by a crowd expecting to hear Matron, or Mrs Sprayspit, give her talk.

"Sit well back," Evie advised when she joined them. "She's got some new teeth and is breaking them in."

There was a dais in front of the rows of chairs and from there, Matron did an adequate job of selling the finer points of the organisation to anyone prepared to give a donation. Dorothy looked around. To her, the audience seemed more like potential clients. Matron thanked everyone for coming and ended by suggesting that they stay to enjoy the treat prepared for them.

"Some of our residents are talented people, as you have seen in the displays of work. Now, we have a singer and dancer with an accompanying pianist who will perform for you. Let me introduce Mademoiselle Evelyn Millepied and Major Giles Snodgrass, DEF, CMC and bar, who will company her on the piano."

In the fifth row back, Sue and Dorothy's incredulous snorts were disguised by polite applause. Mademoiselle Millepied indeed! How like Evie, and as for Giles, was he really a Major or had Evie's imagination been at work?

There was no way to dim the lights but with canvas drawn over the entrance, a slight dimming of the area was achieved. Giles came on to the dais and settled himself at the piano. He waggled his fingers in the air then brought them down with a thump on to the keyboard. Loud chords emanated and everyone sat up to attention. There followed a vigorous intro of some tune everyone recognised but could not name. That done, he started something more lyrical and Evie tripped like a prima ballerina on to the dais, feet at ninety degrees and arms waving like a drowning swimmer signalling for help. She was wearing a shapeless, gauzy, floaty pink skirt and bodice with thin straps over her spare shoulders. When she reached the centre of the space she paused, feet pointing in different directions and hands clasped over her non-existent bosom. As the music began to rise and fall, she began to sing.

Sue and Dorothy prepared to cringe with embarrassment. Instead they stared in amazement. Evie had never sung in the house except when washing up. She would stand at the sink and in a little squeaky voice, give a rendering of all the hymns she knew. As these were of no interest to the others, they never listened to her. Now, she was giving her all, creakily and slightly off key, but there was no denying her heart was in it. Giles accompanied her, after a fashion, and when the duet was over, Evie began to dance. She swayed, she twirled, she pirouetted and high kicked (which wasn't really very high), she scooped low, dipped and reached up in a surprisingly elegant manner. They gazed in amazement for she was really rather good. The audience were overawed, Sue and Dorothy were spellbound. Eighty-two, amazing. It showed everyone what was possible by older people, when others might well have considered them ready to meet their Maker.

Giles did his level best but it was clear he had scant control over his wayward fingers. However, determination and early conditioning saw him through. Finally, when Evie ended her performance with a foolhardy attempt to do the splits, they stood side by side to take a bow. The applause was truly sincere.

As the audience left the pavilion, Sue and Dorothy heard snippets of conversation.

"She was a pupil of Margot Fonteyn, you know. One of the staff told me."

"How old do you think she is?"

"Oh, ninety at least, I should think. Isn't she a marvel?"

"The voice was a bit croaky but what can you expect at that age? What was that song she sang?"

"It was *Beautiful Dreamer* with a bit of *We'll Gather Lilacs in the Spring* tacked on to the end. The poor man lost his way, I think, but she adjusted very well."

Seventeen

After their visit, Dorothy felt less anti the Sunnyside Care Home than formerly. She had noticed a number of residents around the grounds, either ambling along the paths or pushed in wheelchairs by uniformed staff. She had even questioned some and had received nothing but praise and good reports about the place. It was not cabbage and weak tea every day and there was always plenty to do. Evie had taken them both inside the house to view the facilities and they had been impressed. Everyone had their own room and ensuite bathroom. There was a communal dining room, a huge lounge with lots of easy chairs and a games room with a ping pong table, a skittles corner and tables for card games.

"Where do they do their painting and crafts?" Sue asked. "I play the violin but it doesn't always go down well."

"There's another building round the back. It's where I practise," said Evie. "You could play your violin there."

Sue nodded happily. "But is there a vacancy? Would I have to wait for someone to die before I could come?"

"I don't know, dear, but I can ask Matron."

From this exchange, Dorothy was sure Sue would be on the list for a place. If she herself ever chose to apply, she would have a long time to wait.

Back at base, there followed a period of enforced togetherness. Sue was waiting impatiently to hear and Dorothy found the worry over her future robbed her of the ability to concentrate. Neither of them felt inclined to put in the effort of earlier times. There was less sharing, less compromise, no pleasantries and more selfishness. The bare bones of their routine were maintained out of sheer habit and convenience, but it was a bleak time.

Then one afternoon, Evie popped in. "Oh, I say, what a mess, you poor things. But I have news that will cheer you up. I'm engaged. Yes, I know, it's hard to believe, isn't it, but we thought we had better *carpe* the *diem*, 'cos we are not getting any younger."

There was a stunned silence. Dorothy was rehearsing all the comments she might have thrown at Evie.

Sue stood with wide eyes and her hands over her mouth. "Engaged to Giles?" she said.

"Who else, dear?" And the suggestion of triumph in her smile was not lost on either Sue or Dorothy. They were silent for several minutes before they felt bound to congratulate her. For the ten minutes it took to drink a cup of tea, nothing more was said. Then Sue put down her cup and turned to Evie.

"Now Evie, tell us, because we are interested, what is it about Giles that you like so much?"

Evie beamed. "He's such a lovely big man, I love big men."

"Is that all? Because of his size?"

"And because he will look after me. He's very like me, you know."

"Really? Surely not."

"Oh yes, but you don't know him like I do."

"We don't know him at all. In what way is he like you?" Said Dorothy, hiding her disbelief with curiosity

"We have things in common, his music, my dancing. We make a team, a partnership. And he understands me."

Dorothy raised an eyebrow. The man must be a genius if he had accomplished what they had never managed to do in all the time they had known her.

"Do you actually like him?" she said.

"What a silly question. Of course I like him. We have the same sense of humour. We laugh at the same things, just like my Daddy."

Dorothy nodded several times as she noted this, and sat quietly while the conversation moved on.

Sue was being effusive in her encouragement and good wishes. The topic was so all-consuming that the conversation progressed no further. Evie obviously had no interest in her friends' news, except to say that her engagement was good news for Sue because when the marriage took place, the couple would move in together, leaving a room free at Sunnyside.

"You can snap it up if you are quick about it," she said.

Sue lowered her hands to reveal the rapture that thrilled through her. "Oh, wonderful. When is the wedding?"

"We won't hang about. It will be as soon as can be arranged. Everyone is so pleased for us and excited. They don't have many weddings to celebrate."

Dorothy was struggling to look pleased. *Just another thrill on the way to the cemetery,* she thought, hoping her attempt to smile didn't look too ghoulish. Certain random images flitted through her brain. He was so big and Evie was so small. He was heavy and she was skinny, like a deflated balloon; a size eight body in a size sixteen skin. It was all too off-putting. True, they were not getting any younger, but there

wasn't much hope of them getting much older either...
but then, you never could tell.

In a way, she was pleased for Sue, but knowing she
would be left alone when Sue left, brought a tear to her
eye, that Evie did not fail to notice. "Oh Dorothy, I
have never seen you cry out of happiness before.
Thank you for that. You are not such a bad stick after
all, are you?"

Dorothy turned away to hide the withering look that
overtook her features.

They talked it over when Evie left. Dorothy couldn't
contain her opinion any longer.

"I think he has bamboozled her. He wants her to
look up to him, cling to him and think he's a god. You
wait, within months she'll be ironing his shirts. I've
seen it all before. She's got a lot to learn."

Sue replied, "Well, she had better hurry up because
she hasn't got long."

Sue was disgustingly cheerful after that. She would say
nothing critical of the situation. "You know, Dorothy,
Evie was the daftest of us all, yet she has achieved a
secure future in a way we can only envy."

"I don't envy her. She's got to wake up every
morning and see that moustache beside her on the

pillow. It'll remind her of Daddy. In fact, to all intents and purposes, he IS her daddy."

For an instant Sue was puzzled, "Her daddy, what do you mean?"

"Oh forget it. Perhaps he's not such a bad solution for her. Maybe he'll curb her skittish ways and stop her flitting about like a lost moth. She might even grow up."

Jerry fulfilled his promise and the room in Sunnyside soon to be vacated became known as Sue's room. Before she could move in, Evie's wedding had to be arranged. As the bride's closest friends, Sue and Dorothy were called upon to help dress her. Evie had her own ideas, however, and any advice they gave was redundant.

"But you can't wear white at your age. It's inappropriate. A smart two piece in a sober blue would be best," Dorothy said.

But no, Evie had never worn a sober anything and she wasn't going to start now. "It's my first wedding, so why not? And I am a virgin after all."

After all what? Dorothy thought.

But white it was to be, with a veil and all the trimmings. "You may think it's over the top, Dorothy, but it will be such a thrill for the residents. We don't see each other as old and everyone loves a traditional wedding, don't they."

"So what about Giles? Top hat and tails, is it?"

"No, he'll be wearing his khaki uniform and all his medals. I wanted him in a white suit but he preferred his khaki. We are going to walk through an arch of the girls holding their walking sticks aloft, and confetti, and white ribbons on the taxi. All those in wheelchairs have undertaken to decorate them with flowers and ribbons and cook is making a wedding cake suitable for us all."

Dorothy turned to Sue, "That means sponge cake with no nuts so no one will crack their dentures," she murmured. "I bet it will have eight tiers, one for each decade."

Sue gave her a playful slap. "Now, stop that. It's going to be lovely." To Evie, she said, "Who is going to give you away?"

"Matron has agreed to do the honours. And I'll have a ring and a bouquet."

"Don't forget the garter. You can have one of Belladonna's. We've got lots of those, as you well know."

Evie clapped her hands. "Of course, that will be something borrowed. Now I need something blue. Oh, this is great fun."

The Big Day turned out to be fine and sunny. Dorothy dug out an old purple dress and jacket she had worn years ago at another wedding. It was tight around the hips and bust and short by today's standards, but she didn't care for there was nothing wrong with her knees. There was a huge wide-brimmed hat to go with the dress, but she would have to apply a large layer of makeup to hide the bruises on her shins and the varicose veins on her calves because tights would be too uncomfortable in the heat.

Sue wore a fitted dress, also a relic of her younger days, and it was also tight in those places she no longer wished to emphasise. The bust seemed to be in a different place lower down but at least she did have a bust and she hoped the pattern of huge yellow daisies would divert attention from the other deficiencies of her figure. So sad those days were gone. The last time she had worn that dress, she had disgraced herself by barging in on one of Jerry and Flora's anniversary dinners. Their friends came, but they had left her out and she was hurt. Determined not to be ignored, she had drunk several vodkas and then burst into the dining room, much to Flora's displeasure, and gaily introduced herself. Now, she studied her reflection and told herself that was all past history and with luck Jerry would not be around to remember that awful evening.

The excitement in the Home was out of all proportion to the event. There were flowers and balloons everywhere, special food on the buffet, there was juice or tonic water with a slice of lemon if anyone wanted to pretend it was a gin and tonic, and a cheap white wine from the local supermarket for those who could manage something alcoholic. The cake was a picture; Evie had clearly had a hand in its decoration. *Good Luck* in Smarties were pressed into the icing around the side, and there were sequins and pink roses on the top. What lay under the icing was anybody's guess.

Giles had been shunted into the local B&B for the night and would make his own way to the church. When Evie came down the stairs, the crowd of waiting guests gasped. From an ancient old biddy, she had morphed into a fairy in a white tulle ballet dress. She wore blue ballet shoes laced in a criss-cross fashion up her legs. She had a garland on her newly bleached hair and a large quantity of net draped around that floated like a train behind her. Inspired by *Swan Lake,* the only things missing were the wings. She carried a small posy of pink anemones. The intention to descend lightly like a young cygnet was marred somewhat by her clinging with gritted teeth to the banister on her way down. This was no time to trip and fall.

There were *oohs* and *aahs* from the waiting crowd. At the back of the group, Sue muttered to Dorothy, "Who is going to catch that bouquet when she throws it, I wonder?"

"Well, not me if it means shacking up with someone like Giles."

"Now, now, say something nice for a change."

"Sorry, but it is a pantomime, don't you think?"

"You know very well that Evie is guaranteed to put on a show; the theatre is in her blood. Her motto, I imagine, is "better late than never", and she believes in doing everything in her life at least once."

Slightly chastened, Dorothy replied, "Okay, you win."

The bride went off in her taxi to meet her Major to a chorus of well-wishers. Sue took the opportunity to chat to Matron and cement friendly relations with her. Dorothy was at a loose end and went into the lounge to rest her bunions and ponder Evie's popularity. It had surprised her how well-liked Evie was when she herself had always judged her an eccentric dimwit. There was a lesson for her here somewhere. Her own sterling qualities counted for nothing. Her leadership talents were of no account either. No one cared if she had superior intelligence. If she was cheerful, friendly and amusing, that was enough. Did she want to be popular? Just a smidgen would be nice. Trouble was she always forgot to be tolerant when dopes and idiots were around and her critical faculties would not be denied.

It occurred to her that a solitary life lay ahead that she must fill with something. There would be no more spanking, but Sue had succeeded in attracting custom with her wise advice. Something like that would suit and bring in a few shillings to add to her meagre pension. But what was there that attracted the dopes and the idiots and the credulous ninnies too? Fortune telling? Reading palms, tarot card readings, seances? Could she dress up as a gypsy and tout sprigs of lavender around the town? It would be preferable to all that sado-masochism nonsense. She could turn the shed into a consulting room with crystal balls, dim lights, and exotic drapes to hide the holes in the woodwork. At least she would be able to advertise; there would be no more of that hole-and-corner malarkey.

As she sat, running these possibilities through her mind, she began to feel more cheerful, so that when the happy couple returned for the wedding breakfast, she was quite her old self.

The meal was good and went off with a bang, literally, since a few of the balloons decided to burst at the same time. Matron gave a speech, and then those that could still stand jigged about a bit to the 70s number ones. Evie and Giles retreated to their honeymoon in suite number 7, and Sue and Dorothy took a taxi back to Eyesore Towers, now shrouded in darkness.

"Have you got the torch, Sue?"

"Oh golly, in all the excitement I forgot it."

Mellow from that last vodka, Dorothy peered into the darkness, "Never mind, we will just have to feel our way."

Nobody witnessed the amazed look on Sue's face as they stumbled together to the front door.

Eighteen

The next morning Sue told Dorothy that her room at the Home was ready and waiting for her to take up residence that afternoon.

Dorothy seldom felt bad about herself but she did as she watched Sue rush about collecting her things and packing them into bags. It was painful, as Sue was humming happily to herself. It was a bleak moment when she steeled herself to say goodbye and then, in a subdued tone, murmured "Good Luck."

Sue turned to her. "Now Dorothy, I hate to leave you alone like this." Sue's brow was furrowed as she swept a hand over the devastation around them. "But I am sure you understand that I don't want to miss my chance of a room, and a bath. Oh, how I'm looking forward to a bath. We won't forget you. When I've settled in, Evie and I will call to see how you are doing. Alright?"

When Dorothy's girls had finally left her all those years ago, bitterness had surged inside Dorothy. Now, she was battered by experience and had learned lessons. Being deserted yet again, her bitterness was tempered by self-doubt. Was this the inevitable result of all those nasty remarks, those criticisms, that inability to sympathise or tolerate other people's feelings? Of course it was. People had told her often enough. *If you can't be nice, at least be polite.* That was the message she had heard down the years and she had taken no heed, so sure she was right, or truthful or just feeling downright malicious. If no one wanted her around now, it was her own fault.

She stood in the open doorway and watched Sue climb into the taxi, and with a final wave, disappear down the road.

Turning back and picking her way carefully through the debris, Dorothy went through to the kitchen and out of the back door. She walked down to the shed and stood to examine the sorry sight. It stood askew on its moorings, as if some giant hand had pushed it. The side panels had gaps and holes where they had been pushed apart by the storm winds. The door jambs were slightly off kilter so that she had difficulty opening the door but once inside, it looked sound enough, except for the piles of junk they had stored there.

She stood, contemplating the mess, and taking her hands from her pockets, she told herself she was not going to be destroyed by this latest setback. She would not be beaten. Somehow she had to live, and certainly not like a hermit. "I am not a loser," she murmured. "I will pick myself up, dust myself down, literally, and start all over again." The old song echoed in her mind and she began to clear a way through the jumble. A plan was forming. "I'll show them." If she pretended bravado long and hard enough, it might become real. What else could she do?

While Dorothy laboured on her new plan, Sue and Evie lived comfortably in Sunnyside. Evie was already a fixture, with her programme of entertainment firmly established. It took no time for Sue to settle in. Her room was small and spare, more like a cell really, but she had her books, her violin and a few photographs of her poor husband and Jerry as a young lad. She had made up her mind to reprise her role as a sympathetic listener, full of good advice and kindly support. To this end she talked to everyone, one by one, whether they wanted to listen or not. Like a visiting cleric in a hospital, she had a captive audience. Some fell asleep while she talked, others appreciated the attention.

At the end of a month, the two of them decided to call on Dorothy to see how she was coping all by herself in that wreck of a house.

"I do feel a bit guilty, don't you, Evie? We were a team and that dream we had has gone forever."

"Not so much a team, more like a ringmaster with two clowns in tow," Evie replied.

"That's bit harsh, but she did like to crack the whip, didn't she?"

"Well, I heard she was living in the shed and had gone mad, so we must be prepared for anything."

"Who told you that?"

"I met a woman who answered an ad in the local paper. She went for a consultation and was told a load of rubbish about her future. She was told her husband would come into money but he's been dead for years. Oddly enough, two weeks later, I saw her second wedding photos in that same paper. What do you make of that?"

They were going to catch a bus to the Close but Giles had access to a little car and delivered them in style.

What with the wind and rain, the house looked even less inviting than before. There was no reply when they knocked on the scarred front door.

"I bet she's in the shed. Come on, we'll go round the back." Evie grabbed Sue's arm and they made their way around the house to the path down to the shed. Weeds were growing where no weeds should be, and windblown rubbish littered the garden. Some leftover food rotted away in a black bin, accompanied by the feverish buzzing of innumerable flies.

Evie pinched her nose. "Whadda frightful mesh."

They reached the shed. There was a notice on the door: *Madame Fortuna is IN*. They looked at each other and chorused, "Dorothy, are you there?"

The door opened and Dorothy stood before them, at least they thought it was Dorothy. Her hair was greyer and longer and fell loosely about her deeply lined face. There was a bandana about her head, the tail ends of which fell to her shoulders. She had on the largest pair of hoop earrings Sue had ever seen: as least as big as jam-jar tops, and several bead necklaces and pendants, each engraved with mystic symbols and signs of the zodiac. She wore a blouse in some thin material with gilt braid sewn roughly around the sleeves and a crinkly full skirt with a velvet bolero stitched with silver moons and stars.

"Dorothy? Is that you?"

"Madame Fortuna to you, if you don't mind," came the reply.

"We've come to see how you are. We said we would, but it looks as if…" Sue couldn't finish her sentence because she was flabbergasted. Evie took over. "We were worried about you but it seems you are clarified."

"What? Oh yes, after a fashion. Come into my office." Madame Fortuna turned and went inside the shed and they followed. Once there, words failed them.

The inside was hardly big enough for all three and had been transformed into an outlandish space that sparkled with shiny bits and pieces. The walls were covered with multicoloured drapes, hung with several dreamcatchers, and the windows let in only a little light through the purple netting. A small table was covered with a chenille cloth with fringes touching the floor. A large crystal ball sat on the table and on the floor beside Madame Fortuna's chair was a basket containing a Ouija Board, several packs of tarot cards, some crystals threaded on string and a bunch of something that looked suspiciously like seaweed.

"Goodness, how did you manage to do all this?" Evie made delighted little squeaks as she looked around.

"Curtains from the bedrooms here, junk shops, the Indian shop in the High Street and charity shops. I did my research, believe me."

"Oh, we believe you, don't we, Sue?"

Almost bereft of speech, Sue nodded. "Is this how you spend your time, telling fortunes? Do you get many customers?"

"Quite a few. You'd be surprised."

"And do you charge them?"

"Of course. Why else would I do it?"

The two visitors were silent, awkwardly peering into the dark recesses of what had been the potting shed and overcome by the fumes from the jasmine joss sticks.

Evie said, "I imagine you actually live in the house, don't you?"

Madame Fortuna nodded. "Do you want to come in for some herb tea? I make it from the leaves in the garden. It saves buying Typhoo."

There were nods and, backing out through the door and taking a deep breath of fresh air, they made for the kitchen. Madame Fortuna followed after turning the notice to *Madame Fortuna is OUT*.

It was obvious that no cleaning had been done for some time. As well as a thick layer of dust, several books lay about on the worktops. Sue noticed *Palmistry for Beginners, How to Read the Tarot Cards, Psychic Powers* and a thick tome entitled *The Spiritual Life*.

"Well, this is a surprise. Who would have thought that you, our down-to-earth, rational, plain-speaking, no-nonsense friend would end up doing this," she said.

Madame Fortuna had turned back into Dorothy as soon as they were inside the house. Now she shrugged. "What else could I do? I did my research as you can see. It was no more strange an option than turning myself into a dominatrix."

Put like that, Sue and Evie were inclined to agree. In fact they felt a certain respect for Dorothy.

"I couldn't have done it," Sue replied, "and I think you should be proud of yourself."

"Hang on there. It's not easy being a clairvoyant or a psychic anything in this sceptical age. But how about this tea. Grab a stool while I make it."

There was only one stool so Sue wandered around the kitchen, opening cupboard doors and remembering the times they had spent together. The herb tea, when it came, was ghastly, but they swallowed it somehow and then took their leave.

Back in Sunnyside, they were just in time for tea and cake. They sank into the easy chairs with a deep sigh of satisfaction and chose strawberry cheesecake and a cream eclair to go with their Earl Grey.

"Wasn't it awful?" said Sue. "I was so upset. You know, I looked into all those cupboards and there was absolutely nothing. There was only a lump of cheddar in the fridge and I swear the bread in the bin was stale."

"She has lost a lot of weight, from her face especially. I noticed that." Evie wiped a dob of cream from her chin.

"And that shed, with all that garish tat everywhere. What could she have been thinking? Did you recognise the curtains from your bedroom?"

"Yes, I did. She had one of my best scarves round her waist too. It was all too eccentric, although I did think there were one or two nice touches. Do you think anyone is going to take her seriously?"

"It is all too sad for words. No one should have to live like that. She'll starve. We can't stand by and let that happen."

Evie took a sip from her cup. "I can. She's brought it on herself."

Sue gazed at her. "I thought she was the hard-hearted one. How can you say that? She is our friend!"

"You be an angel of mercy if you want. I've got my hands full with Giles. He will leave his feet around for me to trip over. He's got gout and tells me off every time I skip by. I tell him to pull his feet in but he complains about the pain even though I barely touch him."

Sue did not pursue the matter further but thought long and hard on what could be done to help Dorothy, alias Madame Fortuna.

Without a word to Evie, she finally went to see Miss Minnow. "You did an excellent job selling that house to us but now we have a problem."

Miss Minnow pushed her specs higher up her nose and said, "Who are you and what house are you talking about?"

Sue started again, introduced herself and mentioned Eyesore Towers. At once Miss Minnow's eyes lit up. "Ah yes, three old dears took that bl... beautiful villa off my hands."

"That's right. Well, we had a fire."

"You don't have to tell me. I know all about the fire. I haven't seen it but I imagine that is your problem."

"Sort of. You see, two of us have moved out and now only Dorothy is left there with no money and nowhere else to go."

"Which one is Dorothy?"

"She's the one who came to you first. You showed her the house, remember?"

"Oh yes, the lanky one."

"Now, the question is this. Could you sell the house again? I know it's in a dreadful state but there must be someone with money who would take it on, do it up, that sort of thing."

Miss Minnow frowned and bit on the end of her ballpoint. "It wouldn't be easy if it's derelict."

Sue explained that the house was only partly derelict. The second floor was untouched by the fire and the kitchen was usable. "If it was done up like the other houses in the Close, it would make a lovely home."

"Mm, It has some value, of course, even for demolition. Do the three of you want to sell?

Sue gave her a stern look. "I shall make sure they do."

"Then I had better go and take a look and make some kind of estimate. Leave it with me. Is your friend always there?"

"You might find her in the shed in the garden. She's gone a bit weird – the shock of the fire, you know."

Miss Minnow did a double take when she saw Dorothy. *Yes, quite mad*, she thought, for weird was hardly the word for this crazy eccentric female. But she understood the problem and, while sitting opposite Madame Fortuna in her shed, she explained that if Madame/ Dorothy and her friends agreed, they might sell the house.

"You mean put it on the market, with pictures and descriptions?"

"Well, no, actually. It wouldn't do my company's reputation any good to be seen selling it as is. We would keep it under wraps until a suitable buyer comes along."

"That could take years."

"Don't look so depressed. I have contacts. I'll put out a few feelers and we might come up lucky. Of course, it isn't worth as much as you paid for it, but you all might be glad to cut your losses and get rid of the problem."

The idea of selling had only briefly passed through Dorothy's tortured mind. The house was a wreck. It had been a wreck when they bought it, and it was an even bigger wreck now. However, the fortune-telling business was not going well and the thought of some money, any money, was welcome. Why not let this woman have a go, for she herself had run out of ideas. She had wondered about faith healing but the thought of laying her hands on the grubby bodies of some of her clients put her off. There was £3.20 in her savings account and only two carrots in the fridge so what had she to lose?

"I had better show you round," she suggested and led Miss Minnow through the back door into the kitchen.

Not a word was said as they did the tour. Miss Minnow eyed the blackened lounge, the bare roof beams and the extensive water damage on the east side. She picked her way over the fallen plaster board, the broken panels and the fallen roof tiles, then went upstairs, somewhat gingerly, to view the second floor. The bedrooms and bathrooms were almost in their original state, old, stained and ugly.

Once outside, when she had seen everything, she said to Dorothy, "I don't want you to get your hopes up, Dorothy. I'll do what I can, but it may take a while to find a buyer. All I can say is, don't hold your breath. If anything does come up, I'll be in touch." And with these words, she left.

Never in her life had hope risen so high then dropped to zero so fast. Those thirty minutes floored Dorothy. She felt so bad she had to go upstairs and lie down. Nothing had changed. Everything was as it had been, yet as she lay in the stale sheets of her bed, tears flowed onto the pillow. She lay there for an hour. Why bother to get up? Did she have the strength to go on with the struggle? What was the point of it all? A pound here, a 50p there to add to her minuscule pension; it was not a life to look forward to, especially when eighteen months before, she'd had her own cottage and creature comforts enough to satisfy anyone. But she had not been satisfied, had she? What a mistake it all was.

Nineteen

Hunger drove her out of bed, and the need for a cup of coffee and a pee. She shoved her feet into her old slippers and scuffed around in her overcoat. She had slept in her clothes, now all creased, but she gave no thought to what she looked like, didn't even glance in the mirror to un-tousle her hair. She stood at the window, crust in hand, and realised she didn't know what day it was. They were all the same blank stretches of time, interrupted occasionally by some hopeless soul wishing to know what was in store for them.

As she stood chewing pensively, a figure passed by down the path to the shed. She groaned. She couldn't be less keen to spend time poring over somebody's sticky hands. Nevertheless, she could not afford to turn a customer away, so, putting down her cup and cramming the rest of her toast into her mouth, she made for the door to waylay the person before they turned to go away.

The woman was reading the notice, *Madame Fortuna is OUT*. Dorothy approached. "No, she's not. She's IN. Sorry to keep you waiting. I was just checking the transit of Venus. It makes such a difference to how the day goes." Opening the door, she invited the woman inside.

She was a slight, undernourished woman with straggly hair, and an expression of perennial endurance. She gazed curiously around the shed and sat when Madame indicated a chair.

"Now, name first, while I prepare for the reading. You have come for a reading, I suppose?"

"Gloria, and yes."

Gloria sat with her shoulders hunched and hands pushed between her thighs while Dorothy lit the joss sticks, uncovered the crystal ball and sat with her eyes closed and her own hands cupped around the glass. After a few quiet moments she stirred and said, "You are my first today, Gloria. I have to prepare myself for entry into the spirit world. Now, which of my services do you require?" And she listed, with the appropriate costs, the palm reading, the tarot, the tea leaf interpretation, the healing, or the hypnotic transference.

Gloria pushed her two palms across the table, looking fraught and nervous. "I don't want you meddling with my mind."

Madame Fortuna glanced dubiously at her, doubting there was much to meddle with even if she could. "I can assure you, dear, your mind is quite safe. What is it you want me to tell you?"

215

"I want to know if my husband is going to be lucky next Thursday week?"

Madame Fortuna stared at her. "This is a very specific request but I can tell from your aura that you are anxious and your chakras are at sixes and sevens. Your palms will not disclose that sort of information. I must delve into the ball to see what's going on in your life at the present moment."

Dorothy had learned from her customers that people in general were interested in only a few topics. Were they going to get money, be a success, or meet someone who would change their boring lives? This last was the "tall, dark, stranger" need. The teenagers wanted a romance, or failing that, to know if they would pass their exams. People with bellyache wanted to know if they had cancer, and others were worried about nasty surprises coming their way.

Madame Fortuna stared into the crystal ball, muttering what she hoped were mystic incantations. This sad little woman was fearful of something she expected to happen but what could it be? "Your family problems are causing you pain," she ventured.

"Are they? What are they saying about me now?"

"Ah, the mists are clearing. I see you preparing for change. I see upset. Someone is talking to you..."

"Who is it?"

Peering closer, Madame Fortuna frowned. "It could be a man. Or perhaps a woman. It is not very clear. But wait, I see you worried, but all will be well. The change will be good for you," – she glanced down at the calloused hands before her – "because you are a hard worker."

"But will he win?"

Madame looked up, frowning to hide her confusion. "Who?"

"My husband."

So, it was the old hopes of money. She might have guessed. "However, I can't see the significance of next Thursday. Future events often get very misty."

"It's lottery day."

Ah yes, that's it, but I see happier times ahead."

"But is there money? Can you see money?"

"Show me your right hand. Oh yes, the money line is strong. That is a good sign if it is your right hand. "Right to receive, left to leave," that's how it goes, but I can't tell you how much."

A look of disappointment clouded Gloria's face. "So we won't win the lottery then."

"I fear not, but in the crystal ball I see lucky numbers, 30 and 14. You would be wise to try those next time you buy a ticket."

After Gloria had paid up and left, Dorothy sat back and breathed deeply. What a strain. Had she lost her touch? Usually everyone who came had clues she could use to invent a future. If her intuition failed, she often used the horoscopes in the magazines. They were always inventive and worked well when inspiration was needed.

Turning her notice to OUT, Dorothy went back into the house. With five pounds now in her pocket she could go out and buy some baked beans and bread. There were no appointments later in the day so she could sit in the warmth of the public library for a few hours and read the newspapers. She would be in good company for all the homeless tossers, drug addicts and bag ladies did the same.

In the past, she would have been horrified at the thought of spending time in the company of so many of society's drop-outs, but in her most depressed moments she told herself she was almost a drop-out herself. Like them she had no money and was becoming scruffier by the day, worried that she smelled, and hungry much of the time.

To start with she had avoided contact with any of them. They were not her kind of people except for their cheerfulness. They accepted their place at the bottom of society. They were just unlucky, that was why. They were the dregs but didn't seem to care, concerned as they were for survival, the next meal and where to go for shelter.

There was Pete and Joe, Meg, Stoker and others. Some did not interact with the rest but sat, withdrawn and with bloodshot eyes, hardly able to shift from their chairs. And then there was Wilf. He was a bit of a gentleman with a large grey beard and long hair that obscured much of his face. Wilf claimed he had been everywhere and had tales to tell. Dorothy suspected that although he looked aged, under all that hair there was a much younger man. She listened and talked to him but it was not done to get personal so she couldn't ask how or why he had become such a vagabond.

Listening to him and the others made her see how narrow and restricted her life had been. So conventional; so much focus on being respectable, thinking herself so superior to these folks who had nothing but still got by somehow.

They teased her sometimes. "Yous got smashing teeth. Is they false ones?"

Indignant, she said, "Of course not."

"So how d'yer keep them so good?" This was Joe, whose mouthful of stained and crooked teeth appalled her.

"I clean them and go to the dentist regularly."

He looked at her. "Reglar eh? Oo, ain't you posh? I was about ten when I last saw one of them."

"But don't you clean them?"

"I rubs my finger over 'em sometimes."

"You should clean them twice a day."

"Ah see, that's cos you is middle class." He turned to the rest of the room. "She is, ain't she?"

There were grunts of agreement. "Is different for us cos we're lower class, ain't we? Bums, if you like." Once again he addressed the room and this time there were hoots and cheers all round.

For some reason Dorothy felt ashamed and made a mental note to watch what she said, for now she enjoyed being part of the group and didn't want to stand out. The library had become a place of warmth and human contact. Her hours of time alone allowed her to think about why she liked them despite the obvious unpleasant aspects. They had no time for the conventions and were free and unconstrained in their often quaint opinions. They showed an independence of mind that surprised her. They bore the insults and prejudice thrown at them without caring, and were satisfied with little, depending heavily on good or bad luck. Most of all, they lacked money but set no store by it. It meant for them the next meal, or a bed for the night, a bottle of whiskey, and that was all.

All her life she had aimed for respectability but now that aim was pointless.

"You got a place round 'ere, Dot? You don't look like the rest of us," Wilf said to her one morning.

"Like you all, I had a place once."

"Fell on hard times, did yer?"

"I've got somewhere I call home but it's not exactly a palace."

"Squatting, are yer? Not many handy squats round these parts."

Dorothy asked him where he laid his head.

"Here and there. Sometimes, if I've got the dough I get a bed in the Old Crumblies hostel. I've even slept in the graveyard when all else failed. I'll tell you a tale about that. I was there one time and this little chit of a thing danced around me as I tucked into my pasty, singing to herself. I thought she was a ghost but no, real flesh and blood, she was. Mad as a hatter I guessed, bein out like that in the dead of night and in a graveyard too. Not spooked at all. Told me about a job she 'ad to do for someone she was afeared of. Dashed off, cos she was worried this monster person would catch her. I had a little windfall out of that li'll lady but she was a corker, you know?"

Dorothy leaned forward to listen with all ears. "Did you ever see her again?"

"Nah, I moved on. Never stay in one place too long, that's my motto."

He had called Evie a corker, and the monster… well, that would be herself. It was another painful blow that silenced her for the rest of the day.

Dorothy told no one about her failing business and the one time she offered to read old Meg"s palm the woman laughed uproariously. "Ain't no good you looking for my future, ducky. I'm living it now. What about yer own? You got a few more years to fill, ain'tcha?" But Dorothy was coming to the view that she also was living her future for she could see nothing ahead of her at all.

She planned to go to the library more often. It was a shifting group that came and went, some returning to the same place, even to the same chair. She wanted to tell Wilf about Evie and chat to him, form some kind of rapport. He might become a friend. Never in her life had she needed a friend so badly. If they got on well together, he could use one of her redundant bedrooms and save spending money at the hostel. Why hadn't Evie ever mentioned her encounter with him in the churchyard? She knew the answer to that. She would have been scornful of Evie chatting to a dirty tramp, but Wilf was not that at all. He had intelligence and principles. Scruffy he maybe, but no more than Dorothy was herself these days.

He talked of his travels up and down the country but after a while she became curious.

"Don't you have a family somewhere, Wilf?"

"Got one somewhere. Forget where."

How was that possible? "So you have no wife, no children?" She watched a shadow pass over his face. Touchy subject, she decided, so she added, "I was married for a few years."

"That's not for me. Goes on too long. Tried it once but never again. You're allowed one mistake, ain'tcha?"

"But don't you miss family life, home, kids?" Wilf frowned and didn't answer and at the risk of being nosy, she went on. "What about affection, love?"

His face was suddenly sombre and tight. With a brisk movement, he zipped his jacket up to his chin and stood. "Sorry, Dot, I gotta be somewhere. See yer around."

Left perplexed, she wondered why he had been so cagey. A bad experience, perhaps? It was a lesson to her not to invade his privacy in the future.

On his way to the door, Old Meg put out an arm to stop him. "Hey Wilf, you gonna help me with that trolley you found for my bags? Get it outa the canal before some other bod gets it?"

Dorothy saw him nod. "Tomorrow, Meg. I'll do it tomorrow." And he left.

"What's the betting he don't," the man they called JJ said to Meg.

"Nah, he's a good lad," Meg replied, but JJ shook his head.

"He promised to help me when my old Charlie died, but he never turned up. He was a good dog was old Charlie."

Dorothy listened to all this. She couldn't blame Wilf for not wanting to help JJ, who was the smelliest of the crowd. Wilf was a cut above, his own man, with more going on in his head than anyone else in the room. A man who walked alone, like herself, and she respected that.

The next day, the usual crowd were there, including Meg but no Wilf.

She put her money into the coffee machine and took her paper cup to the seat next to Meg.

"Did you get your trolley, Meg?" she asked.

"Nah, the bugger never showed, just like JJ said." Meg let the wispy strands of her grey hair fall over her face.

"Something important must have come up," Dorothy said.

"Oh aye, maybe." She delved into one of the plastic bags at her feet. "Look what I just got from the back of the supermarket," and she brought out a battered shepherd's pie, no longer frozen, with a sell-by date of the previous week.

The next time she visited the reading room, Wilf was not there and neither were any of the others. The room was empty, with newspapers lying undisturbed on the tables. Retracing her steps to the entrance, she was about to ask the woman at the desk where everyone was, when she saw a notice that in her eagerness, she had missed. It read that the library was for the use of readers and not a daily refuge for those not intending to borrow books. She went to the receptionist.

"Have you banned all poor people from the reading room? Where can they go now?"

The woman was excavating her inner ear with a forefinger. "Not my concern, dear. We know who they are and stop them at the door. That smelly lot of drug addicts were stopping respectable people from using the reading room."

"I was one of that "smelly lot" and I don't smell nor am I a drug addict. Many of them were just homeless and came for the company and to be somewhere warm."

"How many books have you taken out in the last month?"

"Well, none actually, but I have done in the past."

"Then you are banned from the reading room as well, but you can search the shelves if there's some book you are after."

The woman's attitude made Dorothy turn away before her indignation burst from her. No Wilf, no old Meg and none of their small band to cheer her up. Her only chance of seeing Wilf again was at the hostel for the homeless. Deprived of yet another element of her life, she wandered aimlessly around the town, hoping to come upon one of the group. They all appeared to have vanished, so, despondent once more, she drifted to the bus stop and home.

There were so few wanting palm readings these days. Had she been motivated she might have honed her tarot skills but she was too lethargic to focus. Her exotic get-up was showing signs of wear but she became less bothered to keep up the pretence of being Madame Fortuna and reckoned she looked more like old Meg every day.

There was an occasional visit from Sue and Evie, but she didn't enjoy seeing them. They were full of the goings on at Sunnyhill and were uninterested in her activities, such as they were. They usually left with glum expressions and the visits became further and further apart.

Twenty

It was some weeks later when Dorothy began to suffer more dizzy spells. Her diet consisted of bread, baked beans and herb tea and she had lost weight and this may have been the reason. Her balance was unpredictable too. It was a perilous business picking her way through the debris still lying around. She hadn't the energy to clear a way through from kitchen to hall and to the stairs, avoiding the slabs of plaster, the fallen beams and tiles. Should she try a walking stick? Certainly not; that was the thin end of a very thick and undesirable wedge.

One day, as she was navigating her way through, she felt faint. Her vision was playing up again and she couldn't tell whether things were near or far. She peered about her, reached out for something to hang on to. Where was the newel post, the banister? Over there? Surely not. Closer then. Leaning towards the banister, she reached out but no, it wasn't where it looked to be. She cast about, sweeping her hands around for anything to hold on to but her flailing hands touched nothing. There was a moment of confusion. *Oh lor, I"m going,* she thought. She felt the thump as she hit the floor but then, nothing.

Minutes later she came to her senses, lying at the foot of the stairs. There was a searing pain in her side, so she lay still for a while. She knew that pain, although this was worse than the wrist, so she knew she had broken something. She tried to turn on to her side, intending to sit up but the pain was so severe she cried out. Not daring to repeat the movement, she lay still. It hurt even to breathe.

The thought that someone might knock on the front door or walk round the back was a vain hope. Her phone was on the worktop in the kitchen, beyond reach. The dizziness returned and she lay, waiting for her mind to clear. She couldn't get up. She couldn't phone for help. She was stuck until someone came. She might have to lie there until the middle of next week by which time she reckoned she would be dead.

She lay for four hours, passing in and out of consciousness, when the phone rang. It rang for a long time then faded as her battery failed. Then the landline in the kitchen rang a few times then stopped. She wanted to crawl, to get to it and tried to turn over against the pain, but the agony was so intense she passed out.

An hour later the landline rang again. She heard it and whimpered. It was getting dark and she was cold. Then about half an hour later she heard voices, first at the front door and then on the path round by the shed. "She's not in there, so where is she?" It was Sue's voice. Then the back door opened and Evie came in, horrified to find Dorothy prone at the foot of the stairs.

"Did you fall downstairs? Oh, you poor thing." She got up and ran to the kitchen. "Sue, she's in here. She's fallen down the stairs."

The ambulance came and Dorothy was just alert enough to tell the medics about her hip. They gave her an injection then trussed her up on a stretcher and took her off to hospital. Sue and Evie wanted to go with her, but decided on waiting until the morrow when she would be able to talk.

"It was that banister. It was always loose. I nearly fell loads of times," Evie said to Sue beside her on the bus.

"I thought Odd Job Bob had fixed that. I wonder why she didn't have a stab at clearing the mess. The whole place is a death trap. I went into the shed. It looks so tawdry without the candles and the glitter. It doesn't look used, you know. If there weren't any customers, what has she been living on?Do you think we should have done more to help? I felt terrible seeing her helpless like that on the floor. Just think, if Miss

230

Minnow hadn't rung, we might never have discovered her."

"So why did she ring you?"

"Because I'd been to see her. She rang to say she had some news for Dorothy about the house but when she didn't answer her mobile nor the house phone she wondered if something was wrong. I had told her that Dorothy was always there."

The bus had reached their stop, and the business of getting off put a stop to further explanations.

Twenty-One

Sue and Evie were troubled with guilt. They had been living in relative luxury while Dorothy had sunk deeper into poverty. They hadn't visited her as often as they should have, nor had they helped with money or food.

Evie had crossed Dorothy off her Christmas card list a long time ago and now had a husband to worry about, so Dorothy's plight had not troubled her overmuch.

As for Sue, she freely admitted that she had behaved selfishly. The thought of being without a roof over her head had made her panic and, too eager to get somewhere safe, she had rushed carelessly away, thinking only of her own problems. However, a broken hip stirred a sympathy for Dorothy that she thought she should respond to. Now that she was securely closeted within the walls of Sunnyside, she was free to acknowledge her selfishness and guilt.

As soon as they heard that Dorothy was alert and feeling better, they hurried to her bedside.

"I warned you about those stairs, didn't I? I'm sure I did, but Sue thinks it was the banister."

Leaning back on the hospital pillows, tired and stressed, Dorothy said, "It was neither. I had a funny turn and just keeled over. Evie was wrong as usual.".

Sue said, "We all risk falling. I'm none too stable myself these days."

"I am so glad you came when you did. I was expecting to give up the ghost. I was planning my funeral. I've got it all worked out."

"Whatever for? You're not going yet."

"I really thought it was wooden-box time for me. I was looking forward to it. It would solve all my problems and no one would miss me."

Immediately the two chorused, "That's rubbish. Of course we would miss you." And at that moment they thought it was true.

Evie, restless as ever, jumped up. "You've got plenty of life in you yet. Seventy-five is no age these days. You are a spring chicken like me, and I'm eighty-two."

After the laughter, Sue reminded everyone that Miss Minnow had some good news about the house and she would visit Dorothy in a day or two.

"What kind of news? For me or for all of us?"

"We have no idea. Should we all come to hear what she says?"

Dorothy had been told that she would have to stay in the hospital for a while. "My hip bone has to mend and they are intent on stuffing me with vitamin pills. I can't go anywhere until I've put on five pounds, they tell me, so she'll have to come here."

"Well, one thing is for sure. There is no going back to Eyesore Towers for you."

Dorothy gave a heavy sigh. "I suppose not. I will get shunted into some cheap council home and lose my independence, my friends and family, and any chance of doing anything interesting ever again."

"I suppose you'll have to make the best of what life deals you," Evie said, rather too contentedly.

"Oh yes, that's easy for you to say." The sharp tone had gone; Dorothy merely looked glum.

They both left then, to make sure they caught the four o'clock bus, leaving Dorothy feeling dejected, and carrying away with them as much guilt as they had arrived with.

A nervous Miss Minnow came, carrying a modest bunch of petrol station flowers. She was solicitous but in a hurry because she hated hospitals.

"I'm so glad to see you are getting better. The sooner you can get out of this place, the better."

"Thanks for the flowers. Sue said you might call."

"Yes, about the house. I've been in contact with a building contractor friend of mine. I told him about the house. Of course, I had to pull out all the charm stops, but he was interested. He liked the idea of demolishing it and rebuilding in the style of the other houses in the Close. The alternative would be to repair and reshape it, keeping the stylistic features, such as they are."

"Is he planning to live in it?"

"I don't think so. He has a mansion up on the Heights. No, he would sell it. It would depend on which was the more economic solution."

For economic, substitute profitable, thought Dorothy. "How much could we get for it?"

"You mean, how much is he prepared to pay for a ruin?"

Sadly Dorothy nodded. "Okay, tell me the bad news."

"Divide what you all paid for it by three."

Dorothy gulped and stared at the wall. "By three. That's as much as I put in. Sue and Evie would get nothing."

"You three would all have to agree to sign the contract. You would each get a third of the third, to be fair, minus the fees."

Dorothy looked morosely around the room. Such a small amount. Would they agree? It wasn't likely. She shook her head. "I'll ask them but I'm not hopeful."

"She came yesterday," Dorothy told Sue and Evie when they visited to hear the news. "She has found a builder interested in the house."

"My word, that was quick. How did she find him so fast?"

"He's one of her contacts. Waiting in the wings, I shouldn't wonder, as the price he is prepared to offer is ridiculously low."

"Is he the only one?"

"There may be others but who knows how long we would have to wait?"

Sue frowned. "That wouldn't be good for you, Dorothy. Where are you going to stay while she hunts for another offer, that may not be any better?"

All three sat in the hospital room, eyes cast down as they thought. When Dorothy had revealed the builder's offer, they had gasped in dismay. All three would lose most of the resources they had put into the house purchase. What they would get from the sale now would be too small an amount to be useful. Even if Dorothy had all of it, there would not be enough to find her a new home.

"There might be enough to pay the fees at the Home and then you could join us. For a while," Sue said. "Until the money ran out, we could be together again as we planned."

Evie pulled a face. "That would mean she would have to have it all. Is that fair?"

Sue rounded on her. "Well, yes, for we don't need it, do we? You have a husband to look after you and I've got my son doing the honours until the day I die."

Dorothy looked from face to face during this exchange but tactfully said nothing. It was up to them to decide, and after much more discussion, they did. They would all sign the contract but Dorothy would have all the money.

When they had gone, she gave a sigh of relief. When she was finally dismissed from the hospital she would go to Sunnyside to recuperate fully, bank the money, then decide what to do.

Twenty-Two

It took six weeks for Dorothy's hip to mend. During that time Eyesore Towers was sold and Matron had agreed to take Dorothy into Sunnyside for a short period. There wasn't an empty room for her but the Home kept one small guest room vacant for visiting family members or emergencies in general. Dorothy was happy with this arrangement. She saw it as a trial period to make sure she wanted to stay permanently. If so, the next death would vacate a room that would be hers.

For six weeks she hobbled around on two crutches, then one crutch, then a walking stick. She practised going up and down stairs and ate three meals a day until her cheeks filled out and sitting on a wooden chair became less painful.

One day, to her surprise, Clare turned up.

"Oh, hello Clare. How nice of you to visit me."

Clare eyed her suspiciously, expecting sarcasm, but the expression that met hers was open and friendly. "I would have come before but it has been hectic at the Hall. How are you?"

"Getting better every day. I've got another two weeks and then they'll kick me out."

"So did you manage to sort out the problem of where to stay?"

"Yes, don't worry about that. I stayed in a part of the house but then this happened." She patted her hipbone. "I've been here ever since. Sunnyside are taking me in for a spell."

"Ah, yes, about that… I want to apologise. I was too rude and off-hand with you when we last talked. I'm sorry not to have been more helpful. It was only later when I got to thinking about it that I realised what a pickle you were in." Clare sat in the chair opposite her and leaned forward.

"To be honest I wasn't too surprised you sent me packing," said Dorothy. "After all, you owed me no favours after the way I treated you and your sister. I've had time to think about all that. I was a real horror, wasn't I?" Dorothy's expression was suitably chastened.

Clare looked at her for a long moment. "It was ages ago. It is true I simmered with resentment for a long time but most of that has melted away."

"I'm glad to hear that. When I think back… Oh, I regret so much and my feelings of regret have got stronger over the years since. For years I let my unpleasant side rule me. You took the brunt of that."

Clare looked down as she listened, then looked up. "I don't think about that time often these days. I suppose it is because I am content. A few memories do stick in my mind. Do you remember the day I fainted in school and you slapped me for making a fuss?"

"Please, don't remind me. I was awful. But you used to hide my specs in the oven, or the fridge. You made me so cross." There was amused glint in her eye as Dorothy remembered.

Clare nodded and smiled. "I remember. Not very imaginative, was it?" They looked ruefully at each other. "You know, Kitty and I used to spend long hours wondering why you were so mean. We never knew, so I was mean back. Silly, wasn't it."

"I'm not sure I knew myself at the time, but when I think back now, I realise I was angry deep down, and I took it out on you two."

"You can say that again. But why angry? Do you know?"

"Now I do. I was brought up plain and poor. I was gawky and I wasn't good at anything. As a role model my mother was hopeless. She upped and died when I was a teenager." Dorothy looked sorrowfully around the room. "You know, nobody liked me at school – they were all well off with successful middle-class parents, living in nice houses, with nice manners. I so wanted to be like them, and you know what?" She looked hard at Clare. "I've spent all my life feeling resentful and trying to better myself and hide my poor beginnings. I only remember one thing she ever said to me. *Never trust a man, because they'll leave you in the lurch.* I did marry but sure enough, within the year he had taken his guppies and gone. His going endorsed all my experience up until then."

"Oh, Dorothy, that is so sad. What about your father?"

"Never knew him, but my mother said he was a gambler and an adulterer. I aimed to give you something better, and turn you and Kitty into good middle class women. I meant to do well by you and Kitty but I failed and now I'm sorry."

Dorothy looked down and fiddled with her pajama top buttons. There was a catch in her voice and her hands trembled. "It's too late now, isn't it."

Clare got up and came to sit beside her on the bed and took her hand. "It's not too late. While you are alive, it is never too late. I guess you never knew how to love. It may be that simple. But unintentionally, you did something for me, you know. You made me strong."

"That is one thing I've learned these last months. It was hard for you and hardship changes a person. It moulds them into something good, or maybe bad. I've seen a lot of that lately."

Clare studied her. "What else have you learned, would you say?"

Dorothy stared at the ceiling for a moment. "I've learned I'm not the only one to have a bad time. I've met loads of people struggling through life as best they can with even less than I had. You never know how hard it has been for them and yet they manage to rub along. When I see how they cope, I can't criticise or blame them. I used to, as you know. I don't think I had a good word for anyone."

Clare took hold of the hand trembling on the coverlet. "I wish you had said these things earlier. We might have been friends. I can see you have changed, Dorothy, and I'm sorry we can't accommodate you at the Hall."

"Oh, that's alright, Clare. I shall go to Sunnyside, meet my friends and do my best to enjoy it."

Clare reached over and gave her a hug. "I do hope you do. And you must come and see us whenever you can." She got up. "It's Frankie's birthday. I've got to get back for the birthday tea. I hope we will see you very soon."

Twenty-Three

"Would you like me to read your future, Mabel?" Dorothy was sitting at a table in Sunnyside with Mabel and her friend, Vera. It was teatime on a Friday afternoon.

"Oh, do you think I've got one?" Mabel was the Grande Dame of the Home. She blinked and looked across at her friend.

Dorothy said, "Everyone has some sort of a future. It may be about tomorrow or next year; who can tell?"

Vera, a handsome white-haired woman in her early seventies, said, "You do know she's ninety- one, don't you."

"Yes, I know, and afterwards I'll do yours, if you like."

"I am not much of a one for that sort of rubbish."

"But I am a professional. I've been reading tea leaves for years."

"That's nice to know."

Dorothy had been in the Home for a week and was getting the feel of the place. She wanted to get to know everyone and this was her way of making the rounds. It was half past four and the residents had drifted into the dining room for tea and cakes. Edie, one of the volunteer staff, was going round with her giant stainless-steel teapot, filling cups. Plates of cake sat on all the tables. Neither Sue nor Evie had yet turned up but she could see Giles at a nearby table with two other men, arguing fiercely, frowning and pointing an emphatic finger at them. Sue was probably practising her violin in the other building and Evie was working on her splits, after her last attempt that had been nothing short of an eyewatering calamity. She still walked as if she had just got down from a fat horse.

The newcomer had noticed that there was little in the way of conversation between most of the residents. Mostly, they talked about their ailments, the state of their bowels or where their pain was worst. To avoid listening again to the minute and disgusting details of Ginny's recent colonoscopy, she had chosen to sit with Mabel.

She reached for her empty cup and prepared to read the leaves, only to find there weren't any.

"Catering-sized teabags," remarked Vera, who was not only handsome but smart as a whippet.

"Then it will have to be your palm," Dorothy said, replacing the teacup and reaching for Mabel's hand.

"This will be interesting," Vera said.

Mabel's reading was mercifully short and after a quick cuppa and a Garibaldi biscuit, Dorothy wandered around, wondering what she could do. It was restful, being waited on hand and foot, but it frustrated her. They even offered to help her shower, much to her mortification. She could read another book, or start a 500-piece jigsaw or wait for a person eager to know their fate via the tarot cards. It wasn't likely that anyone would pass by because most usually took a nap before dinner and the place became abnormally quiet. All her days were the same and she took a lot of walks, which was good for her hip, but she longed for some task, something to occupy her mind instead of idle chat. Her thoughts often went back to her days before her accident, not to the lonely days in the house, but her mornings in the library with all the men and women. Vagrants, homeless, down-and-outs, call them what one liked, they were more entertaining than the residents in the house and many were as old. Wilf figured in those thoughts too and she wondered if he had returned to the area.

She liked the staff in the Home. There were all colours, with different accents and some unpronounceable names, but though they were much put upon, she admired their patience and cheerfulness. They were saints, every single one.

As for the residents, they were a mixed bunch. Some never got out of their chairs, and had to be pushed around. However, she had seen them get up quickly enough when there was a chocolate cake on offer. There were men for whom shuffling from one end of the room to the other was sufficient exercise for the day and others who pretended to be deaf when it suited. There was one chap who declared he had to know what was happening in the world but who habitually read his newspaper upside down. And then there was Lily who spent her time pulling up her jumper to reveal her bosom. Any staff passing would yank it down, saying "Put it down, Lily." She was now known as *Lily Put It Down.* Nobody else took the slightest notice of her.

There were a few men obsessed with cricket, or football, and one or two with plummy accents called Magnus or Quentin or Tristan. Giles was one of these. The women were Felicia, Ophelia or Alicia but they were the most frequent complainers. The tea was weak. The *crème anglaise* was lumpy. The beef stew, to them *boeuf bourguignon*, was over-salted, and why couldn't they have more *pommes frites?* They looked askance at corned beef hash and had never heard of bubble and squeak.

"Can I go out into the village?" Dorothy asked Matron one day.

"Of course you can, dear. This is not a prison."

"Can anybody?"

"Well, no, we discourage those who are not fit enough, but you and your two friends can come and go as you please. Remember, we lock the doors at nine o'clock."

Twenty-Four

With immense delight, Dorothy walked down the gravel drive and out of the iron gates and along the road to the village. She couldn't walk far but she could catch a bus. A new sense of freedom thrilled her and it put a smile on her face. She breathed deeply of the fresh air. The rooms in the Home were too warm and stuffy and the slight chill in the air out of doors was welcome. During her physiotherapy sessions in the hospital, she had been told to breathe, so she did and it made her feel good.

She would never forget those weeks in that hospital, the long hours of lying still, becoming weaker day by day. She would lift up one skinny arm and bemoan her lost flesh. Then there was the sadness to contend with, and with that, a loss of confidence and the fear that she would be trapped forever in this diminished condition. Fortunately it was all temporary. She had always deplored weakness, especially in herself, and now that she was fit and strong again, she did not want to waste her time doing jigsaws or sitting for hours on her backside.

The bus reached the bus station and she alighted. There in a corner, with her bags all around her, she spied Meg. Dorothy stopped in front of her.

"Got any change, love. I could murder a cup of tea."

"It's me, Meg... Dot. Don't you remember me? In the library before they kicked everyone out?"

"Saints preserve us, so it is. You've changed a bit."

"I lost a lot of weight. I was ill."

"Was you now? Sorry to hear that. Where is you hanging out now?"

"Look, come to the café and I'll buy you a cup of tea, and a meal if you like."

Meg sniffed. "They won't let me in there. There's a coffee stall round the corner. Let's go there."

The stall turned out to be a mobile van with a few rickety chairs in front. Dorothy bought two paper cups of strong brown tea and two burgers. They commandeered two of the chairs and Meg arranged her various bags around her. Dorothy looked at the half pint of builder's tea. "This is better than the wishy-washy stuff we get where I am now."

"I've given up breakfast for Lent, darlin', so this will go down a treat. Thanks a lot, Dot," and she laughed.

"Tell me all the news, Meg. Where is everyone I used to know?"

"Here and thereabouts. I see one or two now and again."

"What about Wilf? Did he ever come back?"

"Ah, you was keen on him, weren't you. He's around somewhere. Don't know about the day but he goes to that homeless hostel at night."

"I'd like to catch up with him again sometime."

"Then you need to talk to Eddie. He's the warden of that place. He'll tell you. Tell him Meg sent you," and she told Dorothy where to find the hostel.

Dorothy stood on the opposite side of the street for a few minutes. The hostel had a name over the door: St CRUMBLE'S NIGHT SHELTER FOR THE HOME-LESS. Meg had told her it was known as the "Old Crumblies Hostel" by the townsfolk. It looked grubby and neglected. Next door was a pizza restaurant, with a shoe shop on the other side.

She crossed the road and pushed open the door into a bare office with only a filing cabinet and a counter. All was silent and at first she thought no one was around. Then a large man, a West Indian she guessed, came through a door. He looked at her in surprise.

"We're shut until five," he said.

"Are you Eddie? I'm looking for a friend who stays here sometimes. Can you help me?"

"What's the name?"

"It's Wilf, but I don't know his other name."

"We have a couple of Wilfs but I can't give out details. It's not allowed. Why do you want him?"

"I just want to make contact with him. I knew him some months ago but he took off, and to be honest, so did I."

The man pinched his bottom lip as he thought. "What does he look like?"

"He's elderly with a lot of whiskers and a beard. He's lean and tallish." Dorothy frowned. What else did she know about him? "And he's travelled a lot, by choice I believe, although he hasn't any money to speak of."

"Sounds like Wilfred Morgan to me. You might catch him here but not every night. He helps me out when things get rough. Got the gift of the gab, he has, when he feels like it. I'll pass the word along that you want to see him next time he turns up."

"He'll know me as Dot, from the library."

She got nothing more from him so made up her mind to come back when she could. It might mean missing supper but it would be worth it.

Later in the day, the buses into town were crowded as people went home from work. Dorothy had to stand all the way, and after she had walked to the hostel, her hip hurt. There was a queue outside now, and from across the road she ran her eyes over every face. They were a mixed bunch, mostly men, hirsute, stooping and tatty, and one or two younger men, none of whom was Wilf. Meg was there, the stoutest of the women, and Dorothy wondered how she managed to be so big, on her frugal diet.

When the doors opened, the queue moved inside one by one. Eddie had told her they had to register and pay their pound to him and that allowed them some sort of bunk for the night and use of minimal washing facilities. When she saw the last man had entered, she followed him. Behind the counter, Eddie was occupied and did not recognise her.

"You don't want a bed for the night, surely."

"No, I'm waiting to see if Wilf, Wilfred Morgan, comes in."

"Not so far, lady."

"Can I wait?"

Eddie nodded to a bench on the wall behind her and continued with his admin tasks. The minutes ticked by. One or two more people turned up but Dorothy did her best to be patient. Eddie looked up. "If you've got nothing to do while you wait, give me a hand with these forms, will you?"

Dorothy got up, eager to be useful and for twenty minutes, she happily sorted forms into alphabetical order, and then, suddenly, he was there in front of her on the other side of the counter.

"Got a helper today, Eddie." His voice was as gruff as she remembered.

"A friend of yours, apparently," Eddie said.

Wilf looked curiously at Dorothy.

Her heart sank. *Oh lor, he doesn't remember me,* she thought. "Dot, from the library, before they kicked us out."

Wilf looked at her, a frown on his face until light dawned. "Course, Dot. What are you doing here?"

"I've come to look you up."

"Fancy that. I ain't had that happen for a while."

"But you do remember…" She was going to say "me" but was afraid he would say "no" so she added, "…that time?"

"Guess so. I remember Tall Dotty, but it was many months ago now. How are you doin Dot? We had some grand talks, didn't we?"

"Before you took off and I got… messed up."

Wilf passed over a pound coin to Eddie. "Save one for me, bro," he said. Dorothy thought he was preparing to go and she couldn't let that be the end of everything.

"Do you feel like a cup of coffee or something? I'd like to hear what you've been doing. Eddie will keep a place for you, won't you," she said, turning to him.

They went to the pizza place next door. Having missed supper, Dorothy was hungry. She chose a pizza and invited Wilf to join her. Then they had a coffee and sat talking for a long time. Along the way, she told him about Evie. "She's married now, you know."

"What, not the monster?"

She pursed her lips. "No, not the monster. Giles is a military man."

"That skippy little thing? That follows. It's middle class to a man in those Homes, I reckon."

In the past, Dorothy would have defended the middle class until her last breath, but not now, not to Wilf. She didn't want him to think of her like that. She looked at his worn leather jerkin, his grubby tee-shirt. He travelled freely, as did the middle classes, of course, but he chose his own routes, laid his head on a rough surface at night and ate when and where he could. To her, that was preferable to four-star hotels and tourist groups festooned with cameras, trooping behind raised umbrellas round some well-worn site, the commentary they heard through their ear phones instantly forgotten.

"Tell me where you have been since I saw you last?" she said.

"I took a turn round the Isle of Wight, then on to one of those other islands, Guernsey it was, just to take a look. Not many free spirits there. Lots of people like you, though."

"Like me? What do you mean by that?"

"Well-off old people."

Dorothy spluttered. "I'm not well-off. Once maybe, but not any more."

"That's why your friend was dancing her socks off in the churchyard, I s'pose."

Dorothy's indignation subsided. She couldn't argue with that. Her reaction to Wilf surprised her. Why were the values she had held all her life overturned by this man? Why did she need him to approve of her, a man that a year ago she would have had no time for? She pondered the puzzle all the way back to Sunnyside.

Twenty-Five

Back in the Home, Dorothy said nothing to Sue and
Evie about her afternoon's jaunt. She found them playing cards in the Games room.

"Where have you been? We missed you," Sue said.

"I went into town. I felt a need to get out of this
place."

"We told Doris you played ping-pong and she
wanted to invite you to a game. There is just time
before the trolley comes round." Sue got up and
waved to Doris sitting on the other side of the room.
Mouthing, "She's here," she pointed to Dorothy, who
felt obliged to go over.

Her head was full of Wilf and their talk. Having to
focus on ping-pong, of all things, was an unwelcome
distraction. She picked up the bat on the table; its
familiarity made her pause and remember, so that when
something white flashed by her in a blur and bounced
off the wall behind her, she turned to apologise. "Sorry
Doris, I've had a busy afternoon. Another day
perhaps."

Regular as clockwork, the supper trolley
approached, pushed by Kadie, from Sierra Leone. Hot
chocolate, biscuits and left-over cake were on offer.

Wearily, Dorothy sat and watched the young girl dole out the drinks, all without a smile or a thanks from anyone.

Drinks were slurped and biscuits munched while the chat went on. Felicia was complaining again that her hot drink was not hot, conveniently forgetting that leaving it to cool for ten minutes while she gossiped to Alicia was the reason. Without a murmur Kadie refilled her cup. Felicia looked up but no word was said.

I knew it would be like this, thought Dorothy, feeling suddenly trapped. She had done her best to fit in. From now on, every day would be the same until she was too zombified to care. She could see Sue and Evie happily choosing between Hobnobs and Rich Tea, with great deliberation. *I have to get out*, she told herself, but how and where to? Getting out was no problem as her time here was temporary but would the house sale money run to her renting a flat after she had paid the Sunnyside bill?

She would need something then to fill her time. Perhaps she could volunteer somewhere for a few hours a week. Perhaps Eddie could use her on routine paperwork. That would allow her contact with Wilf when he was around. She would ask when she next went into town.

In the morning, she went to see Matron.

"I feel perfectly well now and I want to leave Sunnyside at the end of the week. Thank you for letting me stay but I cannot exploit your generosity any longer."

Head bowed, Matron was rifling through papers on her desk, checking their content. "Think nothing of it. I am sure your friends will miss you. You understand that we still do not have a spare room to offer you. We almost did but she recovered. I'll let you have the bill on Friday. Where will you be staying then?"

"A friend has found me a small flat on the other side of town."

"I see. Well, we have enjoyed having you and we wish you luck. Give me your new address and if a room becomes vacant, I'll let you know." Matron turned to her work and dismissed Dorothy with a cool smile.

Neither Sue or Evie showed the least concern when she told them. She described her plans but she discerned few regrets in their responses.

"Goodbye, Dorothy. It's been nice having you around," said Evie.

"Hold on, I'm not going until Friday."

"Oops, sorry." She looked at Sue. "There's only us left now. We'll have to get our peace and harmony from Sunnyside."

"I hope you get some where you are going," Sue added.

"That is not what I am aiming for."

"Oh, what are you aiming for?" Sue said.

"I'm not sure I can put it into words. Time, re-evaluation, stimulation perhaps. I don't know."

Miss Minnow had been a godsend. The place she had found for Dorothy was on the first floor of a large house. To call it a flat was an exaggeration. It was more like a room with a bathroom tacked on. An alcove housed a small stove and a sink, optimistically called a "kitchen" by the landlord. But the rent was low, allowing his new tenant to stop worrying about her immediate future.

In the mornings the sun shone straight in through tall windows and the traffic noise from below was muted. Described as furnished, there was everything she would need, so the loss of what was left in Eyesore Towers was no hardship.

An added bonus, that she kept to herself, was the proximity of the homeless night shelter with Eddie, the possibility of a few hours work with him and a chance to catch up with Wilf. It was only a short walk from the flat to the hostel and the town shops.

She waited a few days before going to see Eddie.

"What, you 'ere again? Can't keep away, can you?" And he grinned, showing his lovely white teeth.

"Eddie, I'm at a loose end. I need some volunteer work to keep me occupied, just a few hours a week." She had paperwork in mind as she had done before for him.

"Huh, paperwork is the easiest of my jobs. You don't fancy laundry, cleaning up vomit and disinfecting the latrines, I suppose?" He was looking at her, eyeing her up and down, no doubt thinking she was too old. "I could offer some admin to start with though. Give you a try. What times were you thinking of?"

"Early evenings? I'd like to help with the registration. And I can cook, soups and stews and whatever you like."

His tongue was probing a molar as he thought. "That might help in the winter. I'll give you a go but I can't pay you."

"I don't need paying. I'll do it for free."

He squinted at her and she could see the question in his eyes. He was asking himself why anyone would choose to do the job unless they had to.

The next Saturday evening, Dorothy was behind the counter stapling forms together when she heard a familiar voice.

"You 'ere again. I thought you'd 'ave gone back to your friends in the Home."

"I'm helping Eddie out. I've left the Home and I'm not going back there."

Wilf eyed her solemnly. "Not staying in the hostel, are you?"

"No, I've got my own place now. I can walk there in ten minutes. It's small, only one bedroom so I can't offer a bed to anyone." She wished at once that she hadn't said that. *Tread carefully*, she reminded herself.

"You only need one place. My place is here."

"Yes, of course. I didn't mean…" He turned to talk to another man in the line. "Hiya, Joe, how's tricks?"

"Can't grumble," Joe said. "Who's yer friend?"

Will turned back to her. "This 'ere is Dot. She's helping Eddie out."

To Dorothy, he sounded remote, as if she was no one he knew. There was no hint of their former friendliness. He was not so easy to talk to as before but she could not give up. She had to try to re-establish that easy way. "We go way back a bit, don't we, Wilf? I'm just finishing here. Do you fancy another cup of coffee for a catch-up? I'll tell you all my news and you can tell me yours."

She could see him debating. Surely he wouldn't refuse. Good manners dictated…

"Alright. I've got a few minutes. Half a mo, I want a word with Eddie first."

She waited a good seven minutes. She could see them talking. There were questions and Eddie looked over at her once. There was nodding and shaking of heads and one or two sweeping gestures before Wilf came back. "Come on then,"

With the coffee between them, Dorothy found herself gabbling about leaving the Home, her friends and about finding the flat. She told him where it was.

"You can call in for coffee any time you feel like it."

He didn't look up, just shovelled sugar into the coffee and stirred it round and round without a word.

After a while, she said, "Are you feeling alright Wilf? It's not like you to be so quiet."

"Gotta lot on my mind. Going on my travels again soon."

"Oh, I was hoping we could stay in touch."

"Why's that then?"

She hesitated. "Well. We are friends, aren't we?"

"You and me ain't got much in common now, do we?"

"That doesn't stop us being friends, does it?"

"I don't clutter up my life with things like that."

"Surely you don't think of your friends as clutter."

He heaved an impatient sigh. "I goes travelling. I ain't got time for obligations."

Dorothy looked at him for a moment. "I was hoping we could meet up now and again."

"No." The word came out with some force. "Don't know when I'll be back."

There was a pause while her dismay subsided. "Where will you be heading this time?"

He was avoiding looking at her but let his eye wander around the room. "Haven't made up my mind."

She was uncomfortable. Clearly, she had assumed too much and the little fantasy she had built in her mind over the past months, was just that – a fantasy. Disappointment clutched at her stomach. She had to go. Draining her cup, she said as brightly as she could manage, "Well, I hope your trip goes well." She picked up her bag and within a few minutes they were out on the pavement.

Her voice trembled as she blithely called, "So long, Wilf. See you around." And walked away.

What a fool I've been, she told herself in the ten minutes it took to walk home to her flat. What had she expected of him? A mere friendship would not have provoked the eagerness she had felt. Nothing else? Of course not. Nothing else was possible, but a special friendship, a connection, someone to care about and who might care about her in a companionable way. Wilf was not going to be that.

It took Dorothy a long time to get over what she thought of as Wilf's rejection of her. Like any kind of personal rejection it hurt and led to much self-examination. It had happened again; she was distressed to realise. First there had been her mother's death, then her husband's departure, Clare and Kitty's exodus, Sue and Evie's move to Sunnyside and now Wilf's disappearance and there was no one to blame but herself. But then she asked herself why she should feel this way, at least as far as Wilf was concerned. Surely his lack of the need for human contact was his problem. He had rejected that need, not her, although she had to admit that they made a strange couple. Strange bedfellows indeed! That made her laugh for such intimacy had never been part of what she had wanted.

Why was she beating herself up about him when it was now clear to her that he was one of those men afraid of commitment, who could not cope with obligations. Perhaps for him any human contact was a chore, as were meeting the expectations of others, keeping promises, having to care for someone other than themselves. Did Wilf really find no pleasure in the company of others or enjoy being needed? If this were true, then she felt sorry for him.

Could he go his whole life avoiding any relationship except the most superficial? Who could he turn to when he was ill or in trouble? She should have asked him, but it looked as if now she would never get the chance.

When Dorothy had worked behind the counter for a while, she ventured further into the back of the premises and was upset to find it so bleak and uninviting. Dirt-streaked bare walls, stained paintwork, no doors on some cells. Dormitory bays with six bunk beds had stained rolled up bedding. No pictures on the walls and the loos stank.

She was amazed that Eddie did everything, with no help. "How do you manage?" she asked him.

He shrugged. "People are turned out before nine in the morning, and by noon I've got it all done except for the cooking."

"But why don't the Council put some money in to make it more...welcoming?"

"Don't want to encourage more homeless. It's for the destitute. They don't care what the place looks like."

"What about looking civilised? Couldn't they manage that? Those latrines are a disgrace. Everything seems designed to be as rough and cheap as they can make it."

"If you're gonna try and beautify this place, you're on a hiding to nothing," he declared.

"But that soup or stew you gave them last night made me heave just looking at it."

"Oh thanks. They don't expect four-star meals, just enough to keep body and soul together."

She asked him where he cooked it and he offered to show her the kitchen. When she saw it she was aghast. There was only a small fridge, no freezer, and crates of cabbages, misshapen fruit and veg discarded by the local supermarket, stacked against the walls, with some outside in the sun all day. There was an awful smell of rot and stale food. The great aluminium pans were rimmed with enough grime to poison an army. Eddie clearly did his best but his best was not very good.

Dorothy was reluctant to comment lest he came back with *Do you think you could do better?* All she asked was when the Health and Safety people called.

"When there's no one else they have to see," he replied. "No one wants this place to be a lure for the Great Unwashed of the town."

"Where are you from, Eddie?"

"St Lucia in the Caribbean."

"I bet you wouldn't put up with this in your town."

"Too right. But nobody cares about this lot."

Twenty-Six

The two of them worked well together but it became exhausting for Dorothy when she began to take on extra jobs. Eddie tried so hard and she guessed he was badly paid so she wanted to help. Almost all the rest of her time in the flat, she slept.

Then one afternoon when she was holding the fort and Eddie was in the kitchen, she looked up from the counter and saw him in the doorway with blood dripping from his fingertips.

"Dot, can you take over in the kitchen?" he croaked.

For an instant, she saw him as a blood-soaked zombie approaching her, but when she saw the size of the cut on his wrist, she gasped. Taking the tea towel he had tucked under his arm, she wrapped it tightly around the wound and rang 999.

"I'll do what I can. Don't worry," she said as the ambulance car took him off.

It was devastation in the kitchen with blood everywhere and cut food scattered on worktop and floor. It wasn't easy to see what he had been preparing but there were a couple of hours before the doors opened, so she set to. She cleared and cleaned the sink, swept the floor and wiped all surfaces clean.

Best to start afresh, she thought, examining the boxes around the walls. First, onions, chopped and put into the cleanest pot, then some of every sort of veg she could find. She topped that up with water and added half a jar of gravy granules by way of stock. Left to bubble for long enough, she hoped it would make an acceptable vegetable stew. Then she returned to the office to open the doors and begin registration.

"Hello darlin, where's Eddie? On yer own, are yer?"

"Someone's doin' us proud today. I can smell onions. Thas a treat. Gone mad, has he?"

Since she was alone for the first time, she was reluctant to tell of Eddie's accident. She replied only that he was busy and moved on to the next entrant, grateful for those who shuffled in without a word.

Registration over, she shut and locked the doors, then went to what passed as the dining room. Two big chaps were asked to carry the huge pot in and she ladled out bowls of stew with large quantities of bread on the side.

"Jeez, that was a treat. Give our compliments to the chef," someone said, and there were nods all round the tables. One or two helped her clear up while she took one fellow aside, told him about Eddie and asked him to keep order until she returned in the morning to let them out.

A call to the hospital confirmed that Eddie had lost a lot of blood but they had stitched him up and he was fine. Some cautious doctor, when he learned where Eddie worked, feared infection, even sepsis, and advised an overnight stay. Hearing that, Dorothy decided it was up to her to open the doors at 9am to let people out and then attempt the jobs that Eddie would have tackled.

It wasn't so bad. She suspected the word had got around and the lads, as she now called them, had been on their best behaviour and done the nastiest jobs.

She thought hard about what to cook; some meat would be nourishing, so she rang the supermarket and asked if they had any cheap cuts to spare. When the daily delivery of unsold veg arrived, there was a bag of meat offcuts large enough to feed the men twice over.

That afternoon, after scrubbing the pans of all the dried food residues and tidying the store cupboard, she set about making a hearty beef stew, filling the place with the smell of frying meat, potatoes and herbs. Then she made a whole pile of dumplings. Aware of her predicament, the store had included several out-of-date Swiss Rolls that she was later able to offer as dessert.

"Ma'am, you can stay as long as you like," said one old gent, wiping the gravy from the front of his beard.

"The name is Dot, Charlie, or Dotty if you prefer," she said.

"Right you are, Dotty." He lifted a thumb and smiled at her.

On the fifth day, a man in a suit arrived. He walked in just as Dorothy was bundling laundry into a bag for collection. He laid his large leather briefcase on the counter and frowned. "Who the devil are you? On whose authority are you here, may I ask?"

Dorothy was panting with the effort of the work and paused before she said, "No one."

"I am from the Council, Steve Mucker to you. Are you the woman we've been told is running this place while the warden is away?

"I guess you could say that," Dorothy said. "I'm just helping out till he comes back."

"But you can't do that! Who are you? You aren't on any of our lists.

"I am only doing what had to be done. What's wrong with that?"

"You can't just walk in off the street. It's not legal. I am going to have to report you. What are you, a charity worker or just a public do-gooder. Who is paying you?"

"No one."

"No one? Are you homeless? Are you living here?" His voice rose with his indignation.

Dorothy said, "I'm only doing this until Eddie gets back."

Mr Mucker squared his shoulders. "There will be no need for that. I shall arrange a replacement manager who will take over at once," and he turned on his heel and made for the door.

A few days later Eddie showed up, his arm in a sling. He could do very little, so Dorothy continued as before with the cooking and cleaning, leaving the registration to him. At almost the same time, the replacement manager arrived with a letter for Dorothy containing her marching orders.

Eddie was cross when he heard the news. "Why can't she stay on? She's been a great help. They are treating you very shabbily, he said, turning from the new chap to Dorothy.

The fellow was a lot less of a gentleman than Eddie. He pushed his hands into his pockets."No can do, mate. She has no official status, only an old girl who just walked in off the street and took over."

Eddie had to avert his eyes from the man's mouth where his clackety false teeth sounded like a Spanish dancer's castanets. He said, "Her taking over saved the day for me and for the Shelter. She's proved a godsend. The blokes like her and she cooks good food. She is popular and she's improved this place from a bug-ridden slum to a civilised refuge."

"Well, that's half the problem, mate. Make it a palace and you'll get inundated by all the vagrants in the county. Look, she's gotta go. Maybe she can apply for a job to the Council but I don't hold out much hope of that succeeding. She's too old, for Chrissakes."

Dorothy sighed with resignation when Eddie told her all this. This was another form of rejection but at least she was expecting it. She was downhearted but never-theless had to admit that the job was getting a bit too much for her. She would like a rest, knowing that when 'clacky teeth' left and Eddie was back in harness, per-haps she could continue to help on her original basis.

She slept late, she read the newspapers and a few books, and she went often to the park, where she would sit and watch the young mothers and their little tots on scooters and bicycles. A letter came from the Council a week later that pleased her. In admittedly bald terms it thanked her for the work she had done in the Homeless Shelter and enclosed a modest cheque. It paid her rent for a few weeks but most of all, made her feel appreciated and cheered her no end.

Twenty-Seven

The time had come to catch up with Evie and Sue. She invited them to supper and planned a meal cooked on her single electric ring and the microwave. It would hardly be *haute cuisine* but good enough, leaving them time to talk and renew their relationship as they had not met for a year at least.

She hoped that both women would be pleased to hear from her and sure enough, they replied and accepted at once. As she planned the meal, she wondered if, while being immersed in Sunnyside life, they had ever thought of her. Probably not. Having given her all the money from the ruined house, they must have felt virtuous and promptly washed their hands of her.

When six o'clock on the chosen Tuesday evening arrived, Dorothy heard Sue's voice on the intercom and she buzzed them in. She stood outside her door to welcome them for the first time since their parting. They took their time as they climbed towards her and she was shocked at the changes a year had wrought. Sue had put on a tremendous amount of weight and her hair looked odd. She puffed and panted and clung to the handrail for dear life.

Evie was even skinnier, more wrinkled and her hair was dyed coal black. She barely managed the stick she was using to help her stagger step by tortuous step to the landing. When they reached Dorothy's door, it was a good two minutes before they could speak.

So much for sitting on your backside all day eating biscuits, Dorothy thought. "Come in, ladies." She smiled. "Long time, no see."

Together they took command of the sofa, sitting side by side like Jack Spratt and his wife, leaving her the stool. She poured three glasses of cooking sherry first, then sat looking at her two friends.

Evie spoke first. "You look settled, Dorothy. How do you cope with living in town?"

"I like it. I miss trees and greenery but there is always the park. I walk there regularly and then have a coffee in the café."

"You have to cook for yourself, though, don't you." Evie spoke as if this was an intolerable imposition.

"True. I can't afford restaurants but I can choose what I feel like eating."

"We don't have to bother with any of that, thank goodness," Sue said.

"And how are things at Sunnyside?"

"Much the same. Mabel died. Alicia went a bit funny and punched Quentin. Gave him a black eye.

That was an interesting drama but not much else has happened."

Evie nudged Sue. "Tell her about the heating."

Sue perked up. "Oh yes, they turn the heating on at four o'clock now instead of five."

Dorothy opened her eyes in mock disbelief. "Do they now."

"Yes, and we all have to save water. That's a bit of a nuisance."

Dorothy said, "Mm. Miss Whatsit offered me a room, you know. I imagine it was Mabel's, but I turned it down. I was needed here."

"Oh really? Who needed you?" The emphasis was on the *you* as if this was a most unlikely event, so Dorothy told them the bare bones of her time at the Shelter.

"You are telling us you spend your time with dirty old tramps!" They both shuddered.

"Oddly enough you know one of them, Evie. Do you remember Wilf, the chap you met in the churchyard during your blackmailing jaunt?"

"Did I? What blackmailing jaunt? I've never blackmailed anyone in my life."

Should she tell them about Wilf? He had gone for good and so had Evie's memory, by the look of it. Dorothy turned to look at the window, remembering the last time a month or so ago when she had last seen him. She was walking in the park, along the path around the pond. A lone figure stood ahead, gazing out over the water and with a jolt she had realised it was Wilf. Walking a little slower she approached. Should she speak? She glanced across the pond to see what he was gazing at but could see nothing special. Without a thought, "Hello Wilf," slipped unbidden from her lips. He turned, looked at her, then walked through and past her. Her arm half reached out to touch his arm but then withdrew. No word, no sign of recognition. It was like a stab and she was left standing for a long moment before she continued her walk.

She daren't even try to describe all that to Sue or Evie for fear of tearing up.

They chatted for a while longer, then she invited them to sit at her small table. Evie prised herself upward, using her stick. She been sitting with her knees wide apart, her skirt stretched over them. A pair of woollen socks embroidered with strawberries were pushed into open-toed sandals. She was still skinny but the elegant ballet dancer had gone for good.

Sue had four goes at getting to her feet. When at last upright, she pulled a cardigan tightly around her, and clinging to Evie's arm, took tiny steps towards the table.

Dorothy served them an M & S quiche, buttered carrots, sugar-snap peas and tiny boiled potatoes. In deference to Sue's weight problem, she decided to leave the trifle in the fridge and gave them tinned peaches instead. Because it was a kind of celebration, she opened a bottle of red plonk. There were only two glasses, so she had hers in a cup. The food must have been different from their usual fare for they ate voraciously and at speed, then sat back replete, saying "That was so good, Dorothy."

"You can call me Dot now if you wish – everyone at the hostel does and I've got used to it now."

"Oh, we were terrified to use it when we were in Eyesore Towers. Don't you remember? You came down on us like a ton of bricks," said Sue.

Dorothy looked abashed. "I can't disagree, but I was different then."

"We were all different then, weren't we?" said Evie as her stick clattered to the floor.

"How is married life, Evie? Is Giles treating you well?"

Evie took a deep breath. "I don't like to grumble because he's such a darling of a man and so loving. He's quite my hero - I'm so lucky and being married is thrilling. Not that I see much of him these days. He plays mobile war games with his men friends most days. He's obsessed with *World of Tanks*. Of course, he leaves me his washing and disappears after breakfast for the day. But I get along. Unfortunately, he's not much like my Daddy at all, more's the pity."

Dorothy asked, "Isn't there a laundry service you can use?"

"Yes, but you have to pay extra and Giles turned out to be less well off than he said."

"What about you, Sue?" she said.

"I'm fine, but I've given up the violin and I'm learning the ukulele now. As far as extras go, I have the hairdresser every month but she persuaded me to dye my hair so for a while I went ginger. I wanted auburn but I think she was colour-blind. She asked me if I liked it, and though I was horrified, I said I did. I didn't want to hurt her feelings. I knew it would grow out in the end but it's a lot thinner than it used to be, so I plumped for a wig." She put her two hands on either side of her head and inched the wig a little to the left.

Evie chipped in then. "When Sue did hers, I thought I would too. All the best ballerinas had dark hair, you know."

Dorothy stared at her and thought, *For goodness' sake, what world is she living in?* Here was another colour-blind woman who couldn't tell brown from jet black. She turned back to Sue.

"How about your son, Jerry and Ferocious Freda?"

"He's alright, doing well in the feather factory. Fanatical Flora is busy campaigning for *Save The Bullfrog*. But what do you do, Dorothy, at the shelter place, besides your regular walks?"

"I change wet bedsheets, clean the loos, wipe up sick when necessary, and cook one meal a day for thirty destitute men and a handful of women."

"Oh, I say, that sounds dreadful. Why do you do it?"

"Strange to say, I like the work."

They both stared at her in horror. "That's even worse than what happened to you after the fire." Sue didn't want to relive any unpleasantness so began to reminisce about their time together and soon Evie chipped in.

"Do you remember…?"

"Wasn't that fun when…"

And finally -"Weren't we naive?"

All three talked about Mavis, Miss Minnow and Odd Job Bob and all the men they had got to know, agreeing that despite all, it was an interesting time. They chatted on about the good experiences and the not so good for a long time.

As nine o'clock approached, and mindful of the risk of being locked out, they asked Dorothy to ring for a taxi. She did so with pleasure, glad that at least some of her evening would not be wasted.

As they said their goodbyes on her threshold and began the perilous descent down the stairs, Evie called out, "Perhaps we should have another go, do it better this time. We are older and wiser now, aren't we."

Stunned for a moment while the world stood still, Dorothy said, as mildly as she could manage, "Good gracious, whoever would be daft enough to do that?"

They looked at each other and began to laugh, wildly, helplessly. "What a crazy idea!" spluttered Sue. "Are you mad?"

Dorothy stood watching them descend, their laughter ringing in her ears, then she went inside and shut her door.

END

Printed in Great Britain
by Amazon

39054238R10155